"This novel is a compelling coming-of-age story with a thoughtful, inspiring West Virginia girl as the protagonist. A rarely told story, told well."

—Dr. Carrie Messenger
Professor of English, Shepherd University, Author of *In the Amber Chamber*

"I was captivated by Emily Keefer's storytelling. I enjoyed her creative, detailed story in one sitting. She had me on the very first line. I believe any age of reader will be enticed from page to page as they maneuver the beautifully crafted literary prose. A coming-of-age story of a young girl that overcomes challenges and perseveres as she finds her way in life. I can only hope that there will be more offerings from this talented newcomer."

—Bill Sheehan
Author of *A Tail Among Tales*

"Emily Keefer grabs your heart and won't let go. This story is so profound that it tackles the essentials of everyone's life: finding the true meanings of happiness, love, and faith. Keefer ushers the reader through a series of the main character's crucible events during her adolescence. These events enable her through personal discovery to become honest with herself. What she finds is the truth—truth in finding happiness from a peace within, a purity of love and faith, and the importance of family bonds. This book will change the way you perceive your own life, no matter your age."

—Scott A. Porter
Author of *Here They Come*

"I was lucky, fortunate, and now I'm grateful to have found a new voice, a new writer in Emily Keefer. *The Stars on Vita Felice Court* is an original and fresh story. A pleasurable feel-good read from start to finish. Thank you, Emily, for writing such an enjoyable book. Don't leave us waiting too long for another. The world of books needs you."

—Bill Evans, Author of *Live on TV 3 Palm Springs*

"A lovely coming-of-age story sprinkled with lessons of self-discovery and following your heart. A perfect debut!"

—Bitsy Yates
Author of *Unapologetically Yours*

"Emily Keefer is a shiny new star in the book world. Emily writes with honesty and integrity. Readers will champion her main character, Val Beckley, a high school girl in a small town who struggles with family issues, longs for adventure and searches for answers on a spiritual journey. At its core, *The Stars on Vita Felice Court* is a coming-of-age story about love and self-acceptance."

—Kathleen Reid
Author of *Sunrise in Florence*

THE STARS ON VITA FELICE COURT

EMILY H. KEEFER

VIRGINIA BEACH
CAPE CHARLES

The Stars on Vita Felice Court

By Emily H. Keefer

© Copyright 2022 Emily H. Keefer

ISBN 978-1-64663-601-3

Published by

◀ köehlerbooks™

3705 Shore Drive
Virginia Beach, VA 23455
800–435–4811
www.koehlerbooks.com

"The thing you are most afraid to write,
write that."
Nayyirah Waheed, *Salt*

The Stars on Vita Felice Court is dedicated to each person who
helped me find the meaning
of a happy life.

It is also dedicated to those in the world who are struggling with
having a happy life. Our journeys may not be the same, but I hope
this novel can provide a smile, a laugh, or an insight from the
example of how one person found her happy life in the small and
the simple yet wonderful.

Cheers, my friends and fellow readers, to creating a happy life—
one full of laughter, love, good champagne, and a whole lot of
goodness. It is indeed a journey, but one that is well worth every
high, low, and in between—may the guiding stars lead us to where
we belong and to where we are most ourselves.

Chapter One

"There will be a few times in your life when all your instincts will tell you to do something, something that defies logic, upsets your plans, and may seem crazy to others. When that happens, you do it. Listen to your instincts and ignore everything else. Ignore logic, ignore the odds, ignore the complications, and just got for it."
Judith McKnaught

SUMMER

TOO OFTEN, PEOPLE THINK what has happened to them then becomes their story. This outlook leads to feelings of defeat and disappointment with what your life has become because, for most, life is a confusing mix of the good and the bad. While I could also argue that what happens to someone can, in fact, be their story, the full picture is much, much more than that.

Leaving my family to move across the country was not my story. Coming home was not my story. My story was about the journey of self-love along the way: the daily things that brought me closer to the state of happiness and contentment I'm proud to claim today; the people I met and the things I felt.

My story is the fact that after all that happened, I'm alive, in love, and have learned to truly live in moments that matter, even the craziest of moments. Everything happens for a reason.

June 12

The missionaries told me that it would be a smart idea to document this experience in a journal. I hate journaling, but hey, it's not too horrible when your life is about to change; and plus, I'm imagining this as writing to my future, more intelligent self.

Everyone thinks I'm crazy for moving to Arizona during my senior year of high school. All my friends, my family, and even I know it's a bit crazy based on most people's definitions of the word. Everyone is a bit crazy, though.

No one understands, really, and it's going to upset every single plan I have made for my life—a career teaching dance, never getting married, staying skinny, being well traveled and well read, and getting away from West Virginia.

Sometimes it's hard to imagine leaving.

I told my family about my decision to leave at the exact same time I told them I had decided that I wanted to be baptized into the Church of Jesus Christ of Latter-day Saints. That was not my greatest moment. Telling them that I had made the decision simply because "I know it is what God wants me to do" was not acceptable. The two decisions, being a member of the Church and leaving West Virginia, were in fact linked.

Most of my family refused to say goodbye. They kept saying "See you later." I don't think some of them want to see me later. There's a disconnect and I hate it, but it's for the best. Yes, "see you later" is true; I'll see everyone soon. But I won't be the same girl.

I'm ready for wide-open spaces and new beginnings.

There was a fleeting time when I questioned my decision to leave. Some of their points about the irrationality of it all made sense. I just didn't care what they thought, and I knew I had good reasons for going.

I felt the Holy Spirit, and I'm following it to a better lifestyle with the Parker family. I love them. The members of my new church are also known as the Mormons.

No, not the ones that have multiple wives. I'm so tired of my family saying that. Well, once upon a time they did have multiple wives . . . and then they didn't. The missionaries cleared that up for me when I had questions about it. It was a calling from God at the time, but it ended with modern revelation. I believed that to be true after praying about it.

The missionaries told me to learn and then pray about everything they taught—which I did, relentlessly, and received all my answers, especially that the Book of Mormon was true, and that Joseph Smith restored the true church. My family will never understand that.

But anyway, I'm leaving and joining the Church. I met the missionaries. They answered my prayers. I know Heavenly Father sent them to me. He knows every one of us, and He wanted to help me, even when I was too stubborn to help myself. This will get me out of here and give me a fresh start on myself.

Sometimes I think about what would happen if I would stay. Would I be with Jayce? No, most likely not. Jayce is a fool just like all boys in this town are fools; they want to stay here forever. That is really the only reason he is a fool, but I can't imagine staying here forever.

Well, it's too late now. I don't care much about those silly high school things anymore. I'm going to be a Western girl. The West holds a different culture that I look forward to becoming a part of. Dang, for someone who hates journaling, I sure do have a lot to say.

We are officially leaving in about eight hours for the airport—Mom and me. I have all my things packed up in her Volkswagen Beetle, mostly. I have never packed everything in my room to fit on a plane before. Harder than I thought. Mom is great. Honestly, she is the only one really encouraging me in this journey. It's because she knows the Parker family. She knows about the Mormons, and she knows that they are wonderful people. She knows they aren't "trying to steal me away and trap me in their cult" as everyone else likes to say. Even Jayce feels that way. He could barely look at me when he left today. I tried to tell him I would visit. He is the smartest person I know, but he doesn't understand why I'm so ready to leave. He hugged me tight and left without many more words.

Everything will work out.

Western bound,

Val

Midnight. The wind blowing through sheer curtains in my room's window on Myers Ridge Road. My mother had gone to sleep after we ate dinner. A long day of airport dealings awaited us in the morning.

I would miss home. It did not feel much like home now, but with each goodbye I uttered, this whole thing got harder. *I'm sure it's only hard because this is what the Lord wants me to do. The missionaries were right. Heavenly Father wouldn't have given me this challenge if He didn't know I could get through it. It doesn't mean it's not a challenge, though.*

I opened my Book of Mormon and other scriptures the Parkers had given me. *Another Testament of Jesus Christ. A book of hope.* I opened it to a random section. I did that sometimes, as if the Lord would tell me what I needed to hear if I let Him have control.

I had opened to Mosiah 24:15:"And now it came to pass that the burdens which were laid upon Alma and his brethren were made light; yea, the Lord did strengthen them that they could bear up their burdens with ease, and they did submit cheerfully and with patience to all the will of the Lord."

I took a deep breath in and a deep breath out as I repeated the scripture in my anxiety. *It's going to be all right. The Book of Mormon is true; I know it is. I prayed about it. The Church is true, I can do this.*

That breath led me to pack up the last things in my room. My sock drawer was emptied, exposing the lonely brown bottom. The wind blew again, the stifling air escaping the humidity outside and swirling inside the room as the fan spun. I sat on the floor, folding my clothes and packing my books, slowly. I was not rushing the process; not rushing was something I only did when I needed alone time to think.

Weeks ago, I had put together an album of photos of my friends and family that made me smile. I had so many memories here. I pulled it out of the last drawer in the dresser and flipped through its durable pages. I cried, fiercely. The crying that takes your breath away. *Gosh, I'll miss these folks.* Nervous about the unknown, I questioned God and the impetus to leave. I felt that I had to go but did not understand why.

I got through only half of the photos. I stopped as I landed on a still of Jayce Adams and I at a football game. Freshman year.

I had come out for his first varsity game as a starter on the team. He played an impressive amount for such an important game. I stared into the younger eyes smiling in the photo, both so excited for what high school would hold. I took the photo and held it close to my chest, my tears staining the paper.

After a few moments of reminiscing, I opened my phone and called Jayce. Saying goodbye to him earlier had not been enough, and he could help me sort out my confusion and pain. He answered, his deep, sleepy voice asking what was wrong.

The "boy next door," he lived around the corner from my house down the country roads we called home in West Virginia. His family home was built into the side of a beautiful hill by the river—a home they had built years ago, when we were both small and knew nothing of the other, yet.

The world was less magical and more real now, or at least it sure felt like that these last few months. In the grand scheme of things, that was why I was leaving. I wanted to again be a part of the magical world I knew existed somewhere; it just wasn't here any longer.

Jayce Adams: a left tackle on the Mountain Valley High School football team and an impressive wrestler for the school—a quiet, lovely mess of a boy. He had blond curls and bright eyes that I liked gazing up into. Something in his eyes led me to believe there was more to this fun, easygoing, athletic boy I had known for all these years.

He was a mystery that I might never figure out, but I enjoyed trying.

Jayce made me want to stay. He was content with the beauty and simplicity of the hills and mountains that had surrounded him his whole life, and there was beauty in that perspective. But I was searching for something else. Perhaps Jayce knew more than I, but I was determined to find my truth and explore what the West had to offer.

Jayce and I were never officially a couple. It was one of those situations I consider "complicated." I had always been set on leaving this place one day, and I didn't want anything holding me back. Jayce would never do so deliberately, but I felt as if anything that attached me further to West Virginia was to be avoided. Jayce figured I was playing hard to get. We flirted and became great friends but never dated. We were only juniors in high school. I always thought that if we were meant to be together, we eventually would be. Right now, we still had so much growing to do; maybe one day. I honestly believed in "right person, wrong time."

Jayce and I talked about everything. Some days, when the weather was nice enough to skip the bus from school, we would walk together and talk the entire five miles home. To signify we'd be walking, Jayce would ask, "Race ya home?" to which I agreed—always. We never raced; we were in no hurry. One day, shortly before a spring thunderstorm made its way through the West Virginia mountains, we walked and talked even as it started to sprinkle. I always thought it was similar to a scene in a Nicolas Sparks book, although there was no kissing, intimacy, or drama—just talk about the world, politics, school, the future, and family. Jayce and I talked, walked, and heard each other.

I could say anything to Jayce. As many times as we walked those five miles just to talk to each other, it did not feel like enough. I never got tired of listening to what Jayce had to say either. He did not get the best grades, yet he was one of the smartest people I knew. He knew about the world and things in it but didn't apply himself in school. He hated speaking up, so he failed on participation. Many of his teachers gave quizzes on readings that Jayce never did. Instead, he would watch videos on law, rights, news, and history.

From his family he learned to be an extremely hard worker. I admired everything about him; I appreciated the way he was raised, his values, and his sweet side—even though he tried to be a "man" most of the time and hide that aspect of his personality.

Moments after my phone call that night, he arrived at my window. Sweaty and out of breath, he knocked, waved, and smiled a charming hello. His facial expression changed instantly when he saw mine.

"What's wrong, Val? You didn't sound all right on the phone. I just ran here," he said with a chuckle as the sweat from traveling half a mile ran down his face. He took my hand, looking into my teary eyes. He grinned again to lighten the situation.

"Let's talk on the porch, crazy girl," he said, making me smile. I was an equal mystery to Jayce. He had yet to understand my desire for the wide-open.

I willingly followed him out the window. It was summer on the East Coast, humidity sometimes reaching almost 100 percent. The sticky air clung to my tears as we walked to the front porch. I wouldn't miss this humidity at all—though in an odd way I thought I would miss it completely.

"Why didn't you drive here, Jayce? It's almost eighty degrees and it's 3 a.m.," I asked. Nonetheless, I was immensely grateful he had come.

"I don't know. I didn't really think about it. I just came right away," he responded. "The stars are beautiful tonight, though. The biggest and brightest I have ever seen them. Pretty awesome." I had noticed the stars earlier, but Jayce paid attention to the details. With each thing this boy said and did, I fell more deeply in love with him. *Curse my stubborn ways.*

Despite my complexity, Jayce wanted to be there to hear me out, understand as much as he could, and reassure me that he cared, even though he might not understand.

"You're going to write me when you move to Arizona, right?"

"Of course I will." We both loved letters. I knew he was hiding something deeper beneath the mundane question, the reason he ran to me instead of driving, but I did not pry. I sat in the white rocking chair next to him while the warm, humid Southern breeze curved by us. The tears began to flow, reflecting those bright stars. He tried to wipe the tears dry and make me laugh. He succeeded, and we both smiled at the result.

He could make me laugh no matter what; however, once reality set in and the goodbye period drew near, the tears and confusion returned. I was heartbroken that I was leaving him, and I could tell Jayce was hurting too. He held me silently and tightly as I cried, the two of us completely unsure what the future would hold. An hour before I had to leave for my flight, we parted. I went inside to finish packing, and he ran home. *Everything happens for a reason*, I told myself. *You need a wide-open space, remember?*

Completely alone in my room, I realized I would deeply miss all of this, despite how much I wanted to go. I could have succumbed to what seemed like a simple decision to stay, but instead I ignored my emotions, determined to fly to the other side of the United States— leaving everything behind, including the old Val.

Chapter Two

FAR, FAR AWAY

"Know from whence you came. If you know whence you came,
there are absolutely no limitations to where you can go."
James Baldwin

I FINISHED PACKING just in time for our departure to Dulles International. I heard the coffee maker start brewing, signaling that my mom had awoken. I wanted a cup, but I was not supposed to drink it anymore—one of the commandments that I had promised to follow. The aromas wafted all the way back to my room, but I ignored my craving for the dark, rich goodness.

We currently lived at my grandparents' home. My mom had a new boyfriend, and they had just rented a house together, but that ended up not working out for whatever reason. I had lived here most of my life anyway and did not mind; it was my home.

She knocked on my door. "Good mornin', Val. You ready?" she said with tears in her eyes as she looked at my bags, all packed and ready to be loaded into her small car.

I nodded. "Mornin', Mom. Yup, I just have to load these." I hadn't had an ounce of sleep, and all I wanted was to get in the car and doze on the two-hour drive to the airport—partially because I was exhausted and partially because I did not want to think about what was happening. I did not want to talk. No matter how much coffee I drank, my family knew that certain early hours were off limits for talking to me. I would never be a morning person, especially now, without the help of coffee.

But the deeper reason for avoiding talk was that I did not even understand my feelings. How was I supposed to talk about them? I was excited for Arizona and desperately conflicted at the same time.

I stuck with my decision to not talk much during our trip to the airport. When we left my grandparents' house, I reminded myself that there was nothing for me in West Virginia, and that a supportive church family lay ahead. I immediately started falling asleep as we drove further and further away from the place I called home. We drove away from my school, away my family, and away from Jayce. We flew down the highway to freedom, and I dreamed.

My mother was never like my mom; she always played the role of friend more appropriately. She gave birth to me in a small town in West Virginia before my dad joined the military and raised me until I was a toddler in east Georgia, near Fort Stewart, where my dad was transferred by the Army when the War on Terror began. His company finished boot camp and training and soon after invaded Baghdad with others.

When he returned from his deployment overseas, my mother left our family to go out West with the man she fell in love with when my dad was gone. I did not know at the time that she had fallen in love with someone else; I just knew she was leaving.

The new man was named Richard Parker. He was a Latter-day Saint but didn't abide by the teachings of the Church—he was a "Jack

Mormon," who also fought in the war and was honorably discharged after a severe injury by explosive, receiving a Purple Heart medal.

Soon after my mother left for the deserts of the West, chasing a new life, the rest of us drove north. My father, my younger sister, and I packed our things into the family car, and moved back to West Virginia when I was six. My father received custody and was discharged from his combat medic position to take care of the two of us. My sister, Mia, was only three.

I remember the drive up the coast well. Dad was crying because his wife had just left him for another man. He had no job and would soon need to depend on his family in West Virginia. Dad only had two main family members—his mother, Irene, and his grandmother Irma. They were his main family, with his grandmother Irma being the one to raise him. Irma's husband, Ralph, had died years ago, not long after returning from WWII, and she raised my dad alone, as she had her own children.

Born in 1936, my great-grandmother Irma grew up in a small valley town with one grocery store, and she was employed at the only tailor within miles. Making every meal from scratch, she was proud of how she was raised and raised my dad well in turn. She adored him. I have fond memories of spending time with her and listening to her stories when we visited after moving back home.

My small six-year-old-self tried to comfort Dad during our drive, telling him, "It'll be all right. We'll have a good life being back in West Virginia with our family." He was kind and thanked me by patting my shoulder. I knew he was trying to smile so we would not worry.

Mia would not stop crying quiet in the back seat. A loud toddler, she annoyed me sometimes. Little sisters have that effect on older siblings. Granted, she was just as confused as the rest of us, but she was frustrating my attempt to calm everyone down. Mia was a funny child, and she may have been worthy of several eye rolls during that trip, but she was my sister and I loved her.

My attempt to calm Dad and Mia down consisted of several jokes I thought would lighten the situation, singing songs obnoxiously, and trying to engage them in conversation.

The most peculiar aspect to all of this was the fact that Dad did not lean on his mother and Grandmother Irma when we returned. Instead, the three of us moved in with my mother's parents, Frank and Julia, who were bitter toward my mother for moving to Arizona and leaving us. I did not understand this at the time. Nevertheless, they were excited to have us there. Mia and I were close with Nan and Gramps, and we were happy to be around our family again.

Dad worked with Gramps at his business in town. Once Dad had the money, the three of us moved into a place of our own. I started second grade, and Mia went to preschool. I made sure Mia was okay when we were home from school, acting as an older sister and sometimes a mother. We became close yet still bickered as sisters do. She enjoyed sneaking up on me and making sassy comments every chance she got. She made me laugh, but I had to try and keep a straight face to make her think I did not find humor in her ways.

Years passed with only the three of us in our own little life, and Dad got quite good at being Mr. Mom. I had memories of him taking us shopping with money we didn't have to make sure we looked nice for school picture days. He also always made sure our hair was curled because we both had thin, chestnut-brown hair—straight as nails—and we liked for our hair to look different. Dad could not grasp the concept of how to use a curling iron without leaving a noticeable crease, but I appreciated how hard he tried and how much he loved us.

Each year during the summer months, Mia and I would get on a plane to visit my mom, her new husband, Richard, and the rest of the Parker family in Arizona—growing quite close to her new Latter-day Saint family. Mom and her husband were not a part of the Church, but the rest of his family were. They were always kind, fun, and they treated Mia and I like family when we were there.

I got angry at my mother sometimes for abandoning us, but I always hated saying goodbye to her at the end of our trips. I still loved her and missed her. I knew Mom missed Mia and me too. She called all the time, wrote letters, and when it was time for us to end our visits in the West, she would cry a lot. I did not realize she was fighting an internal battle between her desire for a new life in the West and her love for her daughters.

Eventually, after about four years, my mother left her second husband. She missed us too much, and he did not want to move toward the East Coast so she could be closer to her children. Her love for us carried the day, and we, the victors, shared her relief at being close together again.

In the meantime, my dad was in a new relationship. We had known Renee and her two children since we moved back home to West Virginia. Renee's son, John, and Mia were in preschool together. I was best friends with her daughter, Sarah, at elementary school. Our parents used us as their mail carriers, passing along letters to each other. Connections were made, and they wed when I was in sixth grade.

As every pair of best friends should be, Sarah and I were immensely excited that our families were joining together and that we would be sisters. Unfortunately, after the initial excitement, combining our families turned out to be a horrible experience for me.

Everyone in the family had a hobby, a way to spend their time. I sang in choir during the school day and did my schoolwork and 4-H projects at the kitchen table afterward. After homework I would occupy the back seat of the car, being dragged to everyone else's activities. Dad and Renee did not have time or the money for me to become involved in anything else too time consuming.

I felt lost in the crowd, attending Mia's gymnastics class, Sarah's basketball practice, and John's therapy sessions for his diagnosed autism. I was a tagalong to everything because what other choice did I have? I would bring a book, homework, or something else to work on. I loved the feeling of zoning out with a book. Sometimes I would daydream about being on stage, dancing or singing. I tried not to focus on not being involved in something like my siblings were.

Eventually it made me bitter toward my family, who I felt forgot about me unless it was time to babysit Mia and John, or to do chores. It was not all completely horrible, though; I learned to love cleaning, organizing, thinking, and dreaming. I also loved 4-H. I had that. We only had club events once or twice a month and then camp in the summer, which I looked forward to attending more than did my siblings, who did not like the outdoors much.

A lot of the time, however, I felt as if I was wasting valuable time. My mother, now living back at home, worked two jobs, one as a bartender and another in a medical office. She lived in a small apartment down the road by herself, and Mia and I saw her sometimes on the weekends.

After years of being controlled by my dad and Renee, even though I was a well-behaved teenager who rarely did anything wrong (besides sneak candy from the snack cabinet every so often), I got fed up and decided to move in with my mom right before I started high school.

The conversation came in the form of an argument.

"Hey, Dad, Renee, I want to talk to you about maybe joining a dance studio after school."

"Have you done any research about how expensive that is or how much time it entails?" Renee demanded. "Sounds like a decent idea, Val, but really that's a bit inconsiderate of the rest of the family. Do we have time for the dance classes you want to do? With basketball, gymnastics, and appointments, who is going to take you?"

I sat there, hurt beyond words at how little they cared about what I wanted, and how unwilling they were to make it happen for me.

I walked away and thought for a while. I thought of how unfair it was that they made me the bad guy when I wanted to be involved in something I was passionate about. I thought about how they did not even give the idea a second thought beyond furthering their argument.

I walked back downstairs moments later in anger.

"Dad, Renee, I'm old enough to choose. I have decided to move in with Mom at her apartment."

"You spoke with your mom?" Dad asked,

"No, I didn't. But she has said repeatedly that we are always welcome."

Mia looked at me as I said that. She was playing her video game on the couch in her leotard, waiting to leave for her gymnastics practice.

Dad raged red with anger and most likely pain. Renee stormed off and called me ungrateful. There was a lot of yelling as I packed some of my things for the night. Dad dropped me off at Mom's apartment before Mia's practice. I could tell he was hurt, but I needed to do this if I wanted to be happy and involved in something other than school activities.

It was difficult to leave my dad, even though I was only moving down the road. He had been my rock for so long when Mom was gone, but something in him had changed when he found Renee. I imagined he was tired of being Mr. Mom, so he let Renee, the previously single parent, do the job. I did not want to stick around under those circumstances. I wanted to live my life and find my passion.

After I moved in with my mom, I took the bus to and from school, and I started working. I was home alone after school on the days I didn't work, learning to cook and study by myself. I liked the freedom I had, even though it was difficult to adapt to my new circumstances.

SUMMER: JUNE 13

The hot breeze woke me as we pulled into the Dulles International Airport parking garage. *I'm still so tired.* My mom and I grabbed all my bags, which I was sure would cause an issue when we got to the scales for checked baggage, but I would worry about that when the time came. I did not have time for stress today. *The emotional baggage is enough for now.*

At the check-in desk for Southwest Airlines, I gave the worker my driver's license and flight information. She was unable to find the reservation. *What?!* I was terribly confused, as was my mom. My flight boarded in an hour, and we had no idea where my reservation was.

I zoned out while my mom tried to find the information. *I already said my goodbyes. I can't go back home. I need to leave now before I change my mind. Lady! Please just check my bags and get me on that plane!*

Mom shook me from my short daze. "So, Val, I accidentally took us to the wrong airport. You board at Reagan National in less than an hour. I promise I didn't do it on purpose, even though I really don't want you to go," Mom commented with a slight giggle.

She thinks this is funny?

"Before you start panicking, don't worry. I know you don't want to go home, so I booked you the next flight out of Reagan, which will be about five hours from now. I have to get to work, but your dad will come and sit with you there until you leave. I just got off the phone with him. We'll meet him there. I'm really sorry, Val."

I was stressed and a little angry at this extra obstacle, but I let it go. And honestly, although in the moment it was not funny, we both laughed about it all the way to an old-fashioned diner nearby. We waited on my dad to drive the distance to the airport while she drank coffee, I drank orange juice, and we both ate biscuits and sausage gravy. I could never turn down biscuits and sausage gravy. I was a Southern girl at heart, I guess.

Now I would have to say yet another painful goodbye to my dad. The only other time I had seen him cry was when my mother left him.

Mr. Mom took care of my baggage, which was so carelessly packed and clearly over the weight limit. We sat and talked about life, funny memories, college, dance, and how hot Arizona would be when I got there. The time came to go through security.

"I'm scared for you, Val," Dad told me.

"Why?"

"I think this might be a mistake."

"The Church makes me happy, Dad. It's the truth."

He was silent and he gave me a side hug, brushing the comment off.

"I sure will miss you, Dad," I said. I tried not to let myself cry again. *What the heck, who cares?* I was sad I was leaving my family, and I could be upset and emotional. I could cry. *This is hard.*

"I will miss you more than you know," he said, squeezing me hard and refusing to let go.

After giving him one more squeeze goodbye, barely able to let go myself, I got on my flight to Arizona and my new life.

After I had situated myself on the plane, a woman sat next to me and looked concerned when she saw I was crying. She did not ask why there were so many tears, and I did not volunteer information.

I closed the airplane window shade, bundled up in my blanket, and fell asleep. I could have typed or written something about the experience of flying to what I considered freedom, but I did not know how to put my feelings into words in the moment.

After about an hour of being in the air, the soft voice of the flight attendant woke me.

"Would you like something to drink, ma'am?" she asked.

I shook the sleep from my head. "Oh, yes, please; I'll just take a Dr. Pepper. Thank you."

I still did not truthfully grasp why I could not drink coffee or tea anymore but I could have soda. Nevertheless, I had made a commitment, and I was going to follow through. I drank the ice-cold Dr. Pepper and fell back to sleep for the remaining three hours of the flight.

THE PREVIOUS SPRING: MARCH

Over the years, Mom and I went back and forth from living in an apartment to living with Nan and Gramps for several reasons. Her parents were young and full of life, and I liked very much to be around them. They always made their house feel like home to me, and it was where I had lived for most of my life.

After sophomore year started and I settled into living with Mom, I began dancing at a local classical studio. I was sixteen, and after six months of training, I was told I was ready to do ballet en pointe. This was typically something that girls waited and trained for years to do when starting at an early age. I felt honored; I felt as if I could do anything.

I loved every second of it. By junior year I was dancing an average of twenty hours a week, still working a part-time job, going to school, and even training with the football team to become stronger for dance. I was finally involved in and passionate about something after all those years, and I embraced it fully. I thought I was thriving. I was so dedicated to this extremely busy lifestyle I felt was leading me toward success that I did not have much time for Friday-night football games, pep rallies, spending time with friends, sleeping, or taking proper care of myself.

If I did eat to keep up my energy for a given activity, I would go to the restroom and throw it up when no one was there. I wanted to be perfect. I wanted to be able to dance easier, with no body fat and only muscle. But the lack of nutrients and sleep (lack=none) soon caught up to me.

One afternoon in March after football practice, I was running a bit behind everyone else because my mind was weighing heavily on me that day. Or was it because I lacked the energy and bodily necessities?

As my feet became like weights, the world became less clear—my thoughts soon following. The trees and blaring sun faded and slowed while I collapsed to the ground in a moment I will never truly remember.

Jayce, Thomas, and a few other football guys came to help me up. Most of the guys treated me like their sister. As much as I wanted to be a teammate, I was more to them than that. I was like their strong, feisty, stubborn sister teammate. I liked it that way.

I had not eaten in days, and it was not because the pantry was empty. I told them I was simply dehydrated, and they took me to the weight room where they told Coach to call my mother. He did.

I tried to tell Mom that I was fine, but she drove me to the hospital anyway. She was stubborn too; it was a family trait. Nothing really came of the hospital visit. My mom stood by my side as the doctor told me I had anxiety and needed some rest. *Well, duh.* I knew I needed to make a change, but this doctor had absolutely no clue what was going on with me. I didn't tell my mom, either. It was up to me now. I would fix things on my own.

The conversation we had while leaving the hospital amounted to something hopeful.

"I want to leave, Mom. I want to go on a vacation by myself, away from all of this, on spring break. The Parkers reached out to me recently and said I'm always welcome. Maybe we could give them a call and see if I could visit them in Arizona for a week?" The divorce process had been rough, but the Parkers still tried to stay in contact with us.

"I can reach out to them! I do miss Amelia and Mrs. Parker so much. They're great. Let me see what they say, Val."

They replied happily with eager hearts to have me visit. On spring break a month later, I flew to visit the Parker family, who I had not seen in years. I couldn't wait to get out of West Virginia. It was a short trip, but it would help me heal and figure out what I wanted to do. Or least return home not quite as stressed. The Parker family was the sweetest family I had ever met. I liked them a lot. They were loud, funny, and had a positive outlook on everything.

Before I left, my mom mentioned one sticking point.

"They are Mormons, Val. So they don't drink coffee. It's just a part of their religion. But I talked with Mrs. Parker, and she said that they have a Keurig they use for hot chocolate and cider. She said she would get you some coffee for the machine. She is the sweetest woman alive, I swear."

"Well, that sure is nice of her," I said. "We all know what I'm like without my coffee!"

We laughed. I was in much happier spirits with the trip to Arizona in my calendar. I would only be gone for a week to visit, but I felt like that was the break I needed from everything.

I did not know what to expect. Sandy and Harold—or Mr. and Mrs. Parker, as I called them—were Richard's parents. The two of them were about the same age as Nan and Gramps, maybe a few years older, and they were both retired. Married for forty years, they had three children, Heidi, Amelia, and Richard. I would not see Richard much when I was there, from what the family told me; he was a member of a biker club in Queen Creek miles away and did not come around much. Heidi was a busy, married nurse with three hype children under the age of ten.

Amelia was the younger sister, with a loving and supportive husband. I was closest with her. She had four kids when I came to visit. They were all one or two years apart and under the age of eight.

Amelia and her family, along with Mr. and Mrs. Parker, were at the airport with bells on to welcome me. They had signs to hold, hugs to give, and tears to shed. It was the most warm welcome I had ever experienced, and it made my heart swell.

The Parker family lived remarkably busy lives but still seemed content and full of the energy I wished I had. I wondered what made them this way. *Are they so happy because of their church? Are they happy because they don't feel stuck with a wall of mountains around them?*

I wanted to find out. I asked a lot of questions about their religion throughout the week. One day, on our way to lunch, Amelia told me I would make a great Mormon.

"I just wish that people in West Virginia understood what life was like out here. I feel stuck there. This is like a whole new world, and it is so fun."

"We try to have fun despite the heat."

"I like the heat! I hate West Virginia winters; they're always so long. I really love autumn, but winter isn't much fun," I replied.

She giggled. "I don't like winter either. My kids would love it. They've never seen the snow."

We pulled into the taco shop where we would eat for lunch. We walked in, grabbed food, and sat. She said a quick prayer. They always did that. I bowed my head and listened.

We ate, and I asked questions. She seemed to like answering them.

"What makes you pray at meals like that? I know we should give thanks and be grateful, but I'm curious."

"I personally do it because of the teachings of the Church. Prayer is a commandment from Heavenly Father, and He really listens when we pray to Him, even if it is just to thank Him."

"What else do you do that are commandments?"

"Well, we have the ten commandments just like any Christian religion. And we also don't drink coffee or tea, as you know. We have a family home evening every week to learn about the gospel and the Church's teachings. We don't go out on Sundays. We pay tithing. We attend the temple and go to church. There are a lot of them, but they are all for a reason, and they lead us closer to the Lord."

"The temple, is that the large castle building you were showing me as we drove through town?"

"Yes, isn't it gorgeous?"

"It really is! How many temples are there?"

"In the world, I'm not sure. Let's Google it." She pulled out her phone. The screensaver showed a drawing of Jesus Christ. "The Church website says there are one hundred and fifty temples in operation with a few new ones currently being built."

"Wow. They must be important."

"They are. You have to be baptized to go inside, but it is a place where you can feel so calm, and where it's easier to hear the voice of the Lord. I love it there. I don't go as often as I should, but when I do, I feel at peace. It is also where you make promises to God."

"I could use a little bit of peace and consistency these days!"

We giggled. She knew to an extent what I was going through. *And hey, doesn't everyone need peace in this crazy world?*

"Val, you'd make a great Mormon, you know."

"Oh, I don't know about that." We both laughed again. The conversation was fun and light, but I could tell she was being serious. It was one of those random comments that the other person does not think twice about but which the person whom they relayed it to not only ponders but deeply considers its application.

I wanted to be good at something. Everything I had worked for was crumbling around me at home. I took on too much and it backfired majorly. I typically avoided admitting that at all costs; I didn't want my family to be right. This week was different. The Parker family was calm. I kept asking questions, and their answers made me feel good.

Over the Easter holiday, they took me to the Latter-day Saint temple to walk the grounds and watch the Easter pageant, a live production about Jesus Christ and his life as they believed it to be.

The Parkers had the missionaries meet with me. The two of them had a lot of answers, and they were kind as they explained things that had confused me. According to the Parkers, the missionaries paid their own way to leave their family and come share these answers in

Arizona. I did not understand everything, but I was in favor of what they had to say. I didn't know what I wanted to do; I only knew how I felt. I would be heading home to West Virginia in a couple of days, and they provided comfort before I had to face that reality.

One night, near my departure, one of the missionaries asked me if I would be baptized into the Church. "Val, you have shown great faith in your ability to ask questions, have a pure heart, and a desire to know about the true church," one told me as we gathered in the living room.

"I know this is the true church on earth, and that Joseph Smith saw God the Father and Jesus Christ. I know he was a prophet called of God because I have prayed, read the Book of Mormon, and received my answer. Do you believe that this is the true church, Val?" the other elder asked.

"I do think that I have felt at peace and there have been a lot of answers to my questions."

The first missionary pulled out his scriptures and opened to a verse. "In Galatians 5:22 and 23 it says, 'But the fruit of the Spirit is love, joy, peace, longsuffering, gentleness, goodness, faith, meekness, temperance: against such there is no law.' Do you believe that to be true?"

"I do think that is true, yes."

"The Spirit of the Holy Ghost leads us to the truth. This church is true, and I have prayed about it myself. I have seen its truth through the peace, joy, and love that the gospel has brought me in my own life. I hope you can come to know that same truth through following the promptings that the Spirit is placing in your heart."

I thought about everything weighing down on me when he said that. Home, Arizona—how different those feelings were.

The second missionary said, "Val, we are going to have you pray about this, study, and continue to ask questions if you'd like to."

I asked if they would pray with me before they left. The missionaries agreed and thanked the Parker family for dinner.

Members of the Church always fed the missionaries. We all bowed our heads in prayer.

As the prayer ended, I felt a rush of peace. I cried as I said that I wanted to be baptized. There were hugs, tears, and happiness all around. Mrs. Parker cried the most.

This must be the truth. I feel it. And look how happy everyone is. They would not be this happy if it were not true. I had learned of the importance of being baptized and looked forward to planning that, but I considered how challenging it was going to be. My family would not be happy.

Boy, was I right.

Chapter Three

THE DECISION

*"The straight line, a respectable optical illusion
which ruins many a man."*
Victor Hugo

SPRING: MARCH

AFTER THE MISSIONARIES LEFT, Amelia and her family went home for the night. We were all going to church in the morning.

I reflected on Amelia's statement that I would be a good Mormon. Visions of the Easter pageant, the comforting closeness of the entire Parker family, their love for their church, and all the answers the missionaries gave me raced around my mind. I only had one day to organize my thoughts.

I retired to the room that the Parkers had appointed for my stay, a small casita attached to their home. It was quite peaceful. I heard a gentle knock on the door. Mrs. Parker poked her head in and asked if she could sit with me and chat before heading to sleep. We sat on the couch, both in our night-robes. We just connected. That was how I felt with all of them.

"Is everything all right, Mrs. Parker?"

"Yes, everything is good with me. I just noticed that you were very overwhelmed tonight. I want to help in any way I can."

"Well, if you can tell me the best way to go about telling my family I want to join the Church, that would help." We both laughed. Mrs. Parker, as kindhearted as she always was, looked into my eyes while she held my hands.

"We would like you to consider moving in with us. If you honestly think your family won't support you, and if this is something you want, we want you to know that you are always welcome here. We have loved having you this week, Val. We won't be hurt at all if you decide to go home and figure out life there and come back for visits. We just want you to know that you have a whole support system here if you want to join the Church."

"Oh my, well, I don't know. This has all been so wonderful and positive and overwhelming in the best ways. I know my family won't be happy whether I'm a part of the Church here in Arizona or in West Virginia. I don't know what to do, Mrs. Parker. I really don't."

"Val, that is okay. The Lord doesn't expect us to know all the answers. He just asks us to trust in Him. If you know you want to be baptized into the LDS church, then you just need to figure out what is best for you in your spiritual journey. Let's both get some sleep. Do you still want to go to church in the morning with us? I understand if you'd rather stay at home and think this through instead."

"No, that's all right. I have a lot to think through, but I want to come. I do need some sleep, though. Thank you for talking with me tonight. Thank you for everything, Mrs. Parker. It truly means the world."

"There's no need to thank me, honey. You have been such a ray of light this week. We sure did miss you all these years," she said with tears in her eyes. Mrs. Parker put her whole heart into things. She had steadfast faith and love for her family. "It has been a blessing having you in our home. I'll see you in the morning. My door will be open if you need anything at all throughout the night. Mr. Parker gets up every Sunday and makes pancakes and bacon, so make sure to save some room for that. Love you, sweetie."

"Thank you, Mrs. Parker. I love you too. Sleep well."

Despite needing the sleep that I spoke of, I did not get more than an hour or two after spending most of the night in contemplation. I called Mom. I told her how I felt about the Church, about Mrs. Parker's offer, and expressed how confused I was.

"Well, Val, you know I'll support you in whatever you do. I love the Parkers, and I know they have good intentions and that they love you. What do you want to do?"

"I want to be baptized; I just think it would be hard to do in West Virginia," I said, not having the answers for the rest of the statement.

"You need to do what is best for you, Val. I can tell you the family won't be happy either way."

"I know, Mom." I hated it when I wanted someone to tell me what to do for once and they wouldn't. "All right, we will see. I still have one more day to figure things out. I love and miss you, Mom! I'll talk to you soon. Good night!"

I tried to sleep after that, but I had big decisions to make. *What are people going to think if I move across the country right before my senior year?* My family would disown me if I didn't stay in West Virginia. *Who cares? They aren't the ones who are unhappy right now.* Leaving would change everything, but I would be happy just like the Parker family. I wanted that happiness. I would be baptized, and I would be a part of a church family. I would be where there was no harsh, biting winter. Oh, how I hated winter. I could have a fresh start. I would miss my family, no matter how much they bothered me sometimes, and I would sure miss Jayce, and Thomas, too. I most definitely would not miss walking into Mountain Valley High School every day, caring what people thought of me too much, trying to meet all their expectations. I would not miss the drama and gossip that spread throughout the small town.

I would deeply miss a small amount of people. They would stay connected; I knew they would. *How will I explain this to all my friends, though?* It would probably go something like this: "I'm going to move to Arizona over the summer, be baptized into the Church of Jesus Christ of Latter-day Saints, complete my senior year, and make the most out of a new life away from here." They couldn't say much about that. They all wanted away from West Virginia, too.

I fell asleep thinking, and before I knew it, it was morning, and I smelled the bacon and pancakes being made by Mr. Parker. Amelia and her family were already there, the kids loud and excited in their church clothes. I got ready in my floral dress and neutral heels and headed to the kitchen. I did not make my coffee that morning like I had earlier in my visit. I decided to give it up, according to the commandments the Church asked its members to follow. I was going to be baptized, and I would start living accordingly now.

I had made up my mind. I was going to give it my all, including moving to Arizona.

Chapter Four

THE RETURN HOME

"But people could walk the same road and see different things."
John Hart

SPRING: MARCH

AFTER CHURCH, I WENT BACK to the house with Amelia's whole family, the missionaries, and the Parkers. We ate lunch, talked, and laughed. I told them I had made my decision, and we could figure the details in the coming months, but I had decided to move to Arizona and be baptized. They already knew I had decided to become a member of the Church, but moving out West was something I had decided after everyone went to sleep.

I grinned bigger than I ever had as the kids, the missionaries, Amelia and her husband, and the Parkers cried, laughed, and hugged. There would be a lot to figure out, but I was sure about what I wanted to do.

"Val, we are so thrilled you have chosen to be with our family and be baptized. There are going to be a lot of trials when you return home," Mrs. Parker explained as I folded each shirt I had packed for the trip and placed it in my suitcase. "But I know that the Lord will lead and guide you. Can we have a prayer over you before you leave tonight, for your protection and strength as you return home to tell your family this news?"

"I would really appreciate that, honestly," I said.

I knew the priesthood was restored through Joseph Smith, and that elders in the Church could give special priesthood blessings. The men laid their hands on your head, used consecrated oil when sick or afflicted, and prayed to Heavenly Father for the right words to say.

Mr. Parker and Amelia's husband gave me a blessing, along with the missionaries. I hugged them all, one by one, until everyone had been thanked for my wonderful stay in Arizona. I went to the casita room and finished packing. An hour later, Mrs. Parker knocked as I was placing my last pair of shorts in the suitcase and zipping it up. We headed to the airport.

"Val, we will miss you, but you will be back here before you know it. You can do this. I meant it when I said it wouldn't be easy, but I know in my heart it will be worth it."

"I agree, Mrs. Parker. I'm thrilled, scared, and at peace all at the same time. It will all work out."

"You know you can call me Nan, sweetie, instead of Mrs. Parker. It's up to you—whatever you're comfortable with. That's what all the other grandkids call me."

"I do already call my grandmother at home Nan. What do you think about Gram?"

"Gram sounds perfect."

"I think it will catch on. I love you, Mrs. Parker. Thank you for everything. I can't wait to see you soon for this new adventure."

The night I came home from Arizona to finish the school year and get everything together to move west, my mom called me into her room at Nan and Gramps'. They were out of town for business and would be back later that night.

"I told Nan and Gramps you are thinking of moving to Arizona over the summer."

"I'm moving to Arizona, Mom. I'm so done with this place."

"Well, are you going to sit down and tell them everything?"

"I'm going to try, yeah."

"I love them, Val, but they get upset sometimes since we are all so close. I want to show you something." She pulled out a couple of letters that looked fairly old. "Here are the letters that Nan wrote me when I decided to move to Arizona. They aren't pleasant. But I want these to be a warning of what it may be like once they find out about your decision and why you're leaving. But I also want you to know that you always have family here for you. That is something I have learned."

I took the letters in the manila folder to my room and read them that night. I did not come out when Nan and Gramps got home. I heard them all arguing with Mom in the kitchen.

One of the letters said,

I'm sorry, we simply cannot endure this heartbreak. We are no longer able to be the supportive parents you have known. You have made a horrible decision, and we can't support it. You have left your daughters, your family, and your life. Shame on you. We hope you know we will be there for you if you fall, but we also hope you know that we won't be in contact. We value our relationship with Michael and the girls, and unfortunately you have decided to no longer be a part of that.

I did not know how to react. My heart was heavy; so many of these words felt applicable to my decision to move. Only Mom was going to support me. These letters from so long ago showed that support would not come from anyone else. I had already forgiven

Mom, so my heart broke for her. She had changed and come back to us, but these letters must have hurt her deeply.

Mom knocked and peeked into my room. "Val, Nan and Gramps would like to set up a time to talk to you about all of this."

"The only time I'm really free is the hour between school and dance tomorrow. That should work."

I continued reading until I fell asleep. No more coffee for me when I woke up the next morning, so I brushed my teeth, read my scriptures, prayed, threw on clothes, and hopped on the bus. *Only thirty-two more days of this.*

I put my headphones in, listening to the music while I made up a new dance routine in my head that I would hopefully use one day. Thirty minutes later, we pulled into school. I turned my music up a bit louder and let out a huff of frustration.

During homeroom, Thomas and Jayce seemed especially obnoxious because I did not have my coffee and was not fully awake. We were close friends, so they felt comfortable joking with me.

"Aw, someone is grumpy this morning. Don't you think, Jayce?" Thomas said.

Jayce looked at me and gave me a kissy face. "Yeah, but she looks cute. Where's your coffee? That's probably why she looks like she wants to punch someone."

They both laughed, and I just stared at them. I had no kind words for them this early.

"I'm not drinking coffee anymore, boys. I'm going to be Mormon, and we don't do that."

"Wait, what? Lord, help us all," Jayce said. The two boys and a few others laughed. I'm uncertain about what exactly. It could have been my boldness about the seriousness of religion, or they could have been laughing at Jayce. He was funny even though he made me mad sometimes. And he was right: the coffee thing would take some getting used to.

At lunch I sat with my friends like I did every day. The five of us knew everything about each other: our struggles, our families, grades, crushes, and class schedules—since the sixth grade. Tina, Amber, Erin, and Hannah were sitting, chatting away. Amber and Amanda turned to me. Erin and Hannah hugged me and sat back down, already deep in conversation.

"Wow, you're actually eating today?!" Amber said. "Arizona changed you!"

They did not understand the extent of the problem I'd been having with food. I hadn't told anyone. All they knew was that for once I was actually eating a sandwich and chips instead of a single stalk of celery.

"Yeah, I'm treating myself better. I have something to tell you guys."

"Oh my gosh! You and Jayce are dating finally?" Tina asked.

"No, Tina. We are not. Don't be silly."

"Dang it. Someone is going to snatch him up if you don't, Val!" Tina would stop everything to talk about boys.

"Someone can snatch him if they want to. Geez, I'm leaving anyway."

At that, all four turned and looked at me. "Um, where are you going? And what do you mean *leaving*? You just got back from Arizona this weekend," Erin said. She was always kind, no matter what she had to say. We connected the most. She had a dramatic family situation, and we shared that commonality.

"That's where I'm going. I'm going to go back to Arizona."

"You're moving there?" Hannah asked. Hannah was the smartest one in our little group of friends. She was going to get out of this town and go far in life because she had stellar grades and every college wanted her. Her parents had a fund set aside for her, so all she had to do was get on a plane and go to the school of her fancy.

"Yup, over the summer I'm going to move all of my stuff there and start over."

"Gosh, I would love to do that," Tina said.

"But why are you leaving? Who all is coming with you?" Erin asked.

"Just me, E. I'm going to be staying with the Parker family, the ones I stayed with this past week."

"Aren't they, like, super religious?" Amber questioned. Amber was a track star. She was always running, always icing her knees in class, and we often vented and laughed about our choir group together. We all started off in choir in middle school, and we were the only two to stick with it. She would make it out of here too. She was smart, and she was good at everything she did.

"Yeah, they're members of the Church of Jesus Christ of Latter-day Saints. When I move out there, I'm going to be baptized into their church, too."

"My mom said they are Mormons and apparently they have several wives. You don't want to have to share Jayce, do you?!" Tina joked. Amber, Hannah, and Erin laughed at that. I must admit, I chuckled.

"No, Tina, they don't have multiple wives. That was a long time ago, and they don't do that anymore. And Jayce and I will both move on after I leave. It just won't work out, and besides, I want to get out of here and start over."

"So, let me get this straight. You're leaving all of us here . . . in this stupid town . . . for all of the tan Western boys and a new religion?" Amber said.

"Well, yes, I guess if that's how you want to see it. Listen, it'll be fine, guys. I'm still here for the rest of this semester, and even when I do move, I'll come back and visit."

The lunch bell rang, and we all threw away our trash and headed off to our next classes. Amber and I went to choir. Our choreographer was not there that day, so I led warm-ups, and we went over our first few songs with the dances. Our setup for this spring was a love-themed show. We were going to open with REO Speedwagon's powerful "Keep on Lovin' You," one of my all-time favorite classics. The girls would then sing Bonnie Tyler's "Holding Out for a Hero." It was a cheesy but fun song. That would be followed by an all-boys number where they would sing and dance to Billy Joel's "An Innocent Man." The girls would then follow that up by singing the Dixie Chick's "Wide Open Spaces," another one of my favorites. The closing number was Journey's "Somebody to Love." It would be a solid show, and I looked forward to performing it one last time.

That day we mostly just worked on different voice parts. While the tenors and basses worked to sound more like an actual choir, Amber and I sat on the risers and talked.

"So, this moving thing . . . I have a bad feeling about it. And plus, who is going to be our stage manager next year?"

"I don't know, Amber. I'm sure you can do it. You'd be great!"

"It's just not the same, Val. Have you really thought this out?"

"Yeah, I have. It feels good. I'll miss you guys, but I promise to visit. I just have to get out of here, Amber. And plus, I know the Church is the right choice for me."

"I get it, girl. I really do. But it is your senior year. Don't you want to do that all together? Senior prom . . . senior prom with Jayce," she said as we laughed. "Graduation, senior show choir, senior skip day—I get excited just talking about it."

I took a short breath, thought about how Amber would most likely not understand my feelings about the Church, and I replied confidently. "I think I'd rather take the chance at leaving here while I can, you know?"

"Yeah, I get it. What does your family think?"

"I don't know. I'm sure they're upset. Nan and Gramps want to talk with me tonight before dance. We'll see how that goes."

"I look forward to hearing about that. We all support you, Val, no matter how much of a tough time we give you. We just want you to be happy."

After that, it was our turn to practice our voice part. We switched spots with the boys and gathered around the piano.

On the bus after school, I put my headphones in immediately and took a short nap until my stop. As I walked down the long country road that led home, I went over my schedule for that evening. I had to get a snack and change into my dance clothes once I arrived. But when I reached our driveway, I saw Dad and Renee's car and Mom's car in addition to Nan and Gramps'. I didn't know exactly why they were all there at 3 p.m. on a Monday, but I had an idea.

I walked down the hallway and into the kitchen. Everyone was sitting at the kitchen table, and each of them looked concerned. *This isn't going to be good.*

"Val, we all are here to talk to you," Gramps said.

Nan was crying. "You're not going to make it to dance tonight, Val. This is a serious conversation."

"Excuse me? You can't tell me I can't go to dance. You knew I had an important class tonight. You are all unbelievable," I said harshly. "Mom, can you please take me? This is ridiculous." I was not a disrespectful child, but I did not appreciate when my family treated me as if I had no choice about my life.

"I know, Val. I'm not on their side, but we do need to all talk. I'll take you as soon as we're done here."

Unbelievable. They planned a whole intervention to try and get me to change my mind. What is there to talk about, anyway? I grabbed a granola bar and sat down against my will. I only sat so I could get to dance faster and get this over with. Ms. Justine, by ballet instructor from Russia, would be furious. I was the one of the leads in the upcoming spring recital, and she would not be happy if I was late to rehearsal or, even worse, missed it.

"I can't do this. I can't wake up every morning and drink coffee by myself after all of these years, knowing my granddaughter is going to be a damn Mormon," Gramps cried. Nan walked away.

"Val, we just want to understand why you think this is a clever idea," Renee said.

Ugh. I'm clearly not happy here. I did not answer her.

"Are you planning on going to college out there or something? Because you know by the time you graduate, you won't technically be a state resident yet. You would have to live there for two years," Dad tried to explain.

I loved Dad, but I wished he understood more. "I need to get out of here. That is something none of you will understand. Mom is the only one who knows how I feel. And she is the only one who gets that the Parker family isn't trying to steal me away from you all, no matter what you think."

"Well then, maybe you and Mom can just leave," Nan said as she came back into the room. We all stared.

"Leave where?" Mom asked angrily.

"Out of this house," Nan responded.

"Fine. Screw all of you. Mom, Val doesn't need your permission to leave the state," Mom yelled at Nan and Gramps. "She only needs her dad's permission and mine."

"I'm not giving her permission until she explains this to me," Dad retorted.

I could just punch something, I thought. Instead of punching anything, I stared at them and hoped they would see that this was a positive change in my life.

Several more harsh words were screamed that night. Nan and Gramps took back their threat of kicking Mom and I out of the house, but nothing was the same. Renee and Dad left. I had not convinced Dad to give me permission to leave West Virginia.

At the end of the intervention, when everyone left, I went to my room and fell asleep crying. Crying because I had missed a crucial rehearsal, and because all I wanted was to move to Arizona already. I would have to explain my absence to Ms. Justine. *What am I going to say? "Sorry, my family hates the fact that I want to move across the country and join the Mormon church, so they held me hostage in my kitchen to tell me what a horrible idea it is."*

Was it as crazy as it sounded in my head? It didn't seem crazy last week when I was with the Parkers. It felt real, and I wanted more of that. I would not let anyone stand in my way.

I went to sleep angry and even more determined to convince Dad to let me go to Arizona for my senior year. I was going to be Mormon either way, but I wanted to leave, and no one understood how trapped I felt here. I woke up the next day, did not talk to anyone, and did what I normally did since returning from spring break: ate breakfast, read the Book of Mormon, prayed, rushed to get ready, got on the bus and ignored everyone, got to school, and put on a happy face until it was time to go home. When I stepped off the bus, I called Dad.

"Hi, Dad. I would really like for you to consider giving me permission to move to Arizona and live with the Parkers."

"Val, we talked about this last night. No. You can do whatever you want when you are eighteen, but until then, you are staying here and completing school."

"But, Dad, I hate it here. And plus, I'll turn eighteen during August of senior year. They start school there two days before my birthday. I can't miss the first week of senior year just because you won't give me permission."

"Then don't go, Val. It is obviously not meant to be."

"So, you're saying everything I felt while I was there during spring break just wasn't meant to be? No one understands how I feel. I have two options in my mind, Dad. I can stay here for senior year and let this stupid town continue to suck the life out of me, or you can give me permission to leave a few weeks before I turn eighteen so that I can start my senior year in Arizona on time, and I'll be happy."

"I think we all believe the grass is going to greener on the other side, Val."

I was quiet for a moment. "Well, maybe it is going to be greener. It won't be perfect, but I'll be happy. Doesn't that matter to anyone?"

"Let me think about this, Val. I'm not going to easily give my daughter permission to join this new family."

I didn't think much of the new-family comment. I wasn't abandoning my family. I was simply becoming a part of another one in addition—a church family that would love and support my decision.

"Are you coming to visit this weekend?"

"Yeah, I have dance rehearsal all day Saturday, but I'll come stay with y'all this weekend."

"Alright, Val. Talk to you then."

I went into the house and into my room to change for rehearsal and unpack my things from school. As I turned the corner to my room, I saw Nan sitting on my bed, rummaging through my set of scriptures that the Parkers had sent home with me so I could keep up on my studies. All the letters that Mom had given me were sprawled out on the bed, too. Nan was angry and crying when we made eye contact. She just sat there and stared at me. I walked past her and put my backpack down. She left the room. I closed my door behind her and got ready for dance.

I laid down to take a quick nap while I waited for Mom to avoid Nan and Gramps when he got home. I had no interest in talking to them if they had nothing better to do than rifle through things that didn't belong to them.

Dance rehearsal came and went. When Saturday came, I woke up for our last rehearsal before spring recital. I put on my tights, leotard, warm-up pants, and a light jacket. It was April now, but it was still chilly on some of these early mornings. I tied my hair into a tight bun. I was so used to it being in a bun that did not move for hours that it felt odd to wear my hair down.

I was used to a lot of things. I was used to my bed, my home, the back roads, the dance studio, my school routine, and my friends. *Should I still try and convince Dad to let me go? It should not be too hard, and once I do convince him, I won't regret it. I can get used to*

new things. I can get used to a new bed, unfamiliar dance studio, a
new home, and new friends.

I went into my room, packed a bag to stay with Dad and Renee for
the rest of the weekend, and drove to dance practice. After rehearsal,
when Dad and I got home, I made what I thought was small talk,
grabbed a snack, and sat on the couch.

"So, have you thought about letting me go to Arizona?"

"You know what, Val? I don't want to talk about it anymore. I'm
done. Go ahead and go if you want."

I just sat there, not sure what I felt as Dad withdrew upstairs. I
got in the shower and read my Book of Mormon before bed, opening
to my favorite scripture that the missionaries had shown me. It was
the First Book of Nephi 3:7.

"And it came to pass that I, Nephi, said unto my father: I will go
and do the things which the Lord hath commanded, for I know that
the Lord giveth no commandments unto the children of men, save
he shall prepare a way for them that they may accomplish the thing
which he commandeth them."

I know I'm supposed to go to Arizona. I don't really understand it
all yet. I wish I did, but I just need to have faith. The Lord will provide
me a way. Everyone is so upset about it, but they will understand one
day.

I texted Mrs. Parker and Amelia to let them know that Dad had
officially given me permission to come to Arizona. I fell asleep right
after and slept until the sun rose in the morning.

I did not have anything to do for once on that Sunday. I woke up
and spent the morning with everyone—Dad, Renee, Mia, John, and
Sarah. They all talked so generally and passively that I could tell they
were avoiding the fact that they thought I was stupid for deciding to
move to Arizona.

Even my sisters and I had lost touch after I moved in with Mom a few years ago. I knew we would reconnect later, but we had nothing in common right now. It was the same with everyone. *I have nothing in common with anyone anymore besides the church members I met in Arizona. I just need to get there, and then everything will be great.* It wouldn't be perfect. I knew that. Everyone acted like I didn't. *I don't believe in perfection on earth. What is perfection, anyway?* But I would not feel trapped there. I knew it would be *better.*

After spending Sunday with them, I headed back home to get ready for my week, which flew by, as did the next. The same routine followed every day: sleep a little bit, get on the bus, get through the school day, go home, and get ready for dance, and do it all over again. The only breaks in routine were the spring recital and the show choir performance. Those were fulfilling, but I remained focused on where I was going.

Weeks passed by, and then I was within reach of leaving for Arizona—my fresh start. School was out, and I had my guy friends over from the football team for dinner after practice the afternoon before I left for my new journey. Jayce, Thomas, and a few others came by to eat and say "See you later." Mom's boyfriend, Paul, even stopped in on his way to work to wish me luck and give me a hug before I left. He was genuinely nice, and he was good for Mom, despite their current difficulties. I appreciated that he cared enough to stop in.

Nan and Gramps came home from work and loaded up their bags for a beach trip with Mia and our cousin Kim. Mia and I hugged goodbye, and I squeezed her tight. Kim and I hugged and wished each other the best. Gramps hugged me and cried harder than I had ever seen. Nan hugged me, cried, and said, "Have a nice life." It sounded so final.

After that, I had some time to pack. My girlfriends stopped by after rehearsal and gave me gifts, tears, and hugs. I reassured them I would be back soon.

"I may hate it here. But you guys are my best friends. I just need this fresh start. But I'll never be able to replace y'all," I said to them. We said our goodbyes.

Dad, Renee, Sarah, and John came last. Dad's goodbye was the hardest. We hugged and cried for about twenty minutes before he walked to the car. And then we had to do it one more time before I finally flew off on my adventure, filled with relief and uncertainty.

Chapter Five

THE BEGINNING

"There is strange comfort in knowing that no matter what
happens today, the Sun will rise again tomorrow."
Aaron Lauritsen

SUMMER: JUNE 13

WHEN THE PLANE'S ENGINE woke me up, I could not hear. I pinched my nose, closed my mouth, and blew air through my ears so they would pop. A flight attendant taught me this simple trick in my childhood, when I was flying to and from Arizona to visit my mom with Mia. I remember those trips together fondly. We would fly to Mom, just the two of us, eating peanuts and drinking soda with flight attendants who treated us like princesses. This time I was completely alone, and it was very different.

"The temperature is a whopping hundred degrees, the skies are clear, and the sun is shining here in Phoenix," our pilot announced. "Thanks for a great flight, folks, and welcome to spring in Arizona! Thank you for flying on Southwest. We hope you have a great afternoon. Come back and see us soon!"

I smiled as I grabbed my bags and shuffled out with the other passengers. Since departing, I had mostly forgotten about my sadness, and I ran to greet my new family.

Jayce and I sent letters to each other once a week. If I sent my letter out by Monday morning in time to catch the mail truck, it arrived to him by Wednesday if I was lucky. He usually wrote his letters on Wednesday nights after football practice, and if he sent them Thursday morning before his mail carrier came, they would get to me in time to send another the following week.

The letters usually held questions about how life was going for the other. I told Jayce I was getting used to the Arizona heat, and he was beating the humidity on the East Coast. Summer was ending there, and Jayce would be playing football soon. I knew the frequency of our letters might dwindle. I would be starting school and getting used to more new things, and he would be involved with sports and school. Through our continual letter writing, Jayce and I had become quite smitten with each other. I missed him.

I missed everyone back home, but after meeting the new people from my new church, I was able to find friends. My first night there, the entire girls' group from the ward—that was what the sections of church members were called—all got together for an ice cream social to welcome me. It was starting to feel comfortable.

But then the situation with Jayce came to a crossroads.

Dear Jayce,

I hope this letter finds you well. I'm missing the Friday night lights at Mountain Valley, and the chilly nights that we used to spend talking about life. I even miss homeroom and the class periods we had together. I'm living a good life here, learning new things, meeting new people, and I'm loving the weather. The mountains, the sunsets, and the chill before the heat hits the valley every day is something I have been enjoying. I hope school is going well for you, and I hope football is going well also. I miss you, and your sweet smile. I hope Thomas is doing well. Send my love to him. I'm loving going to church out here. I wish you had come with me. I think you might enjoy it. And I sure would like to be able to see you every day. I miss our walks home from school the most. I'm sure I'll be back to visit soon. Sending hugs, kisses, and love. I miss you, my dear.

Love always,

Val

Jayce's response broke my heart, but I knew it was for the best. I remembered the time we sat in his driveway after a failed freshman football game, talking nothing of the game but instead of life. The memory passed quickly as I opened his letter.

Dear Val,

Thank you greatly for your letter. I always look forward to hearing from you. I miss you terribly, and I don't know if I can do this. I don't understand why you needed to leave so badly in the first place.

I want to be with you, and that can't happen while you are in Arizona. I know you have always had a heart for adventure, finding freedom, and exploring, but you could have had that here. I just don't understand. I hope you know I love you, and I always will—I really mean that. I just can't do this. You can always call or text me if you need anything at all. I hope you love Arizona and that it is all you expected. You deserve the best, and all the wonderful adventures. I can only hope it leads back here.

I can't do long distance. I'll always be here and will always be thinking of your sweet heart and all the good thoughts and times we were able to spend together.

Love always,

Jayce

I read his letter and cried. I reached out to everyone else, my girlfriends and my family, often, but I had lost Jayce. He would always be my friend, but I could not be with him. I would have to love from a distance, as would he.

A few weeks later, I got invited to a pool party. It was nearly 100 degrees outside. Jane, Darin, and Kat—all members of the Church—invited me over to Darin's parents' house. I asked Mrs. Parker if I could go. I called her Gram now. She answered yes without hesitation.

We pulled up to the house, an old rancher turned modern—my dream. It was beautiful; there was delicious food cooking and lemonade made for guests. We all said hello to his parents, who were noticeably in love. It was a such a strong household. I was not used to seeing that. There was always an issue, a fight, a lust for control in my family growing up; yet this family and the others I had met so far seemed free and full of joy. I wanted to feel like that.

We all jumped in the pool, and shortly after our swimming and talking, Darin's brother Mitch showed up. There was a bit of tension in the room when he arrived. I learned later that night that everyone except for Mitch was a practicing member of the Church. He was a baptized member and grew up in it, apparently, but did not "abide by the teachings of Christ," as his parents said. He was cute and kind, and he needed a good friend.

I went home that night happy and in good spirits after being with my friends. I said good night to Gram and Mr. Parker and got ready for bed. While brushing my teeth, I thought about journaling. I had not committed to it like the missionaries had suggested. *I really don't like journaling.* I lay in bed thinking and checking social media networks. *Maybe if I type, journaling would be easier.* I did a quick web search for personal blog websites. *Perfect. Typing is so much better.* I did not know where I learned to type fast, but I always had. I took advantage of that and decided to blog rather than write in a journal where my handwriting would be neat for two sentences and then suddenly indecipherable.

First Post: July 10, 12:40 AM

This time four weeks ago (WV time, 3 AM) I had just said goodbye to Jayce on my front porch. I was loading my things into the car and starting my new journey. We stay connected, but it is just not the same after what happened.

I have gotten so much done during this time, and I'm incredibly grateful for everyone that has helped me. I'm blessed to have them and for Heavenly Father's unconditional love for me. This journey may not be the easiest, but there's always a light at the end of the tunnel. I'm grateful that I can chase my dreams and follow the plan that the Lord has for me and to see light along the way.

I decided to start a blog. I think it will be great to have this to look back on and see where it goes. I'll mostly be posting daily blogs, lists, quotes, things to remember, etc. One of my favorite quotes from Pinterest this week: "If you want something you've never had, you'll have to do something you've never done." That speaks volumes to even the trivial things in life. Even starting a blog!

Trust in the magic of new beginnings

Signing off,

Val

I got up to use the bathroom before I went to sleep. When I came back to bed, I decided to write another post. I had a lot on my mind.

Daily Routine for the Rest of Summer: July 10, 12:49 AM

-Morning prayer and scripture study of the Book of Mormon

-Wash face, prepare for the day, dance to music (hey, I may even become a morning person)

-Nutritious breakfast

-In order to feel accomplished, I'll complete everything on my to-do list

-Shower, say my "good nights" and "I love yous"

-Blog

-Night prayer and short scripture study

New Day, New Thought: July 11, 10:29 AM

As I'm blessed to have another day on this beautiful earth, I reflect on why I'm here. I'm here because Heavenly Father has a plan for me to prosper, to help me become worthy of entering the temple, to inspire people, and to chase my dreams. I'll do my best to keep that in my mind as I take the hardest steps of my journey in AZ. Stay focused, but don't forget to have fun (sometimes I forget to have fun). Enjoy life as it comes to you.

It may be hard, but it will be worth it

Bye for now,

Val

Sacrament meeting, Sunday school, and Young Women—or church—all began at 11 AM for our ward. There were so many members in Arizona that we had an assigned time and section in which to attend church. It was three hours long. Sacrament meeting was a big gathering where worthy members took bread and water in remembrance of the Savior. There were talks, prayers, and hymns sung. I loved the structure of everything in this church; it seemed complete. It provided comfort, answers, and organization.

When the last hymn sung in sacrament meeting rang to a close, we moved on to Sunday school. After a talk by a brother in the ward about following the commandments, I began to think of my journey thus far. I zoned out while listening to the congregation sing "The Spirit of God":

"The Lord is extending the Saints' understanding,
Restoring their judges and all as at first.
The knowledge and power of God are expanding.
The veil o'er the earth is beginning to burst."

How lucky I am that all of this happened to me. I'm out in Arizona, beginning a new life—a life I didn't even know I was missing until now. The Church is true. This gospel is true. I can't wait to say I'm a member of the Church of Jesus Christ of Latter-day Saints. The last verse of my favorite hymn began as I came back to reality and joined in with my new church family:

"How blessed the day when the lamb and the lion
Shall lie down together without any ire,
And Ephraim be crowned with his blessing in Zion,
As Jesus descends with his chariot of fire!"

I got chills.

As the song concluded, a missionary recently returned from Chile walked up to the pulpit and said a prayer that the Lord might bless the rest of the Sabbath day and that we would learn a great deal in our classes to follow sacrament meeting. Missions in the Church for males, and to a lesser degree women, were a commandment from God. The prophet said that it would help them to become better disciples of Christ and better parents and spouses one day. They sent in their application, and the prophet prayed over where he/she was to be sent, and then over the decision to learn a new language. After that, the missionary prepared to be worthy to enter the temple— the house of the Lord. They would be sent to a missionary training center, and then off to their designated location for eighteen months to two years to serve and preach the gospel. They paid their own way or received help from the Church to go, and they followed strict rules. It was a huge sacrifice, yet all of them said it was worth it.

The missionaries in Arizona told me all this when I was confused after our first meeting. One of them was from Utah and the other one from Idaho. "How did you end up here?" I asked a year ago. They told me that it was a calling from God. I was intrigued and felt like they had been sent to me.

The pianist started playing to dismiss people to their next classes after the prayer concluded. Everyone who worked here had a job outside of church. Doctors, secretaries, teachers, lawyers—the parts they played here were callings from the Lord. So, everyone from the pianist to the bishop had been called of God and did this out of duty and love for the gospel. I hated that my family kept calling it a cult. It was not a cult. People happily volunteered; God called them to these positions to help others. But the Lord would bless my family. They would understand eventually.

I shook a few brothers' and sisters' hands and went to Sunday school. I sat in the front because I had more leg room and I liked being up front. I was the new girl, but I had never been shy, and I was not going to start now. The Sunday school teachers seemed to like that I sat up front. They liked how much I volunteered. A lot of the other kids, mostly teenagers, did not take part much. They were used to this, while it was new and exciting to me. I could not see myself feeling anything less than thrilled to be a part of this.

The recently returned missionary, Kirk, sat next to me. He was cute and had given his entire talk in Spanish. It was customary for missionaries returning home from their missions to bear testimony of the truthfulness of the gospel. If they learned another language while they were gone, they usually testified in that language. Since Church missionaries followed strict communication rules, and were dedicated and called servants of the Lord, they did not date. Now that Kirk was back, he was reentering the dating world.

"Hey, you're Valerie, right? The new girl from western Virginia who is getting baptized?"

"Hey, Kirk! Congrats on returning from your mission. Your testimony was great. And great prayer today, too. Also, you can call me Val; everyone does—Val from *West* Virginia."

"Val sounds good. And I'm sorry about the mix-up. I have never been out of the West besides my mission, I didn't realize it was a separate state. Does that happen a lot? What is it like?"

"Yup," I said with a grin. *What do these kids learn in history class?* "Ever since the Civil War. And yes, it happens all the time. It's mostly the same as Virginia, just a bit further north. Lots of mountains, creeks, and rivers. It is beautiful in its own way, much different than here." I laughed.

"Hey, a few couples are coming out on Friday for a group date. Would you like to come with me? It will be casual and fun! We're grabbing some food, watching a movie at a warehouse that my dad owns, and skating."

"Sure, that sounds fun! I would like that. Here's my phone number so you can send the details when it gets closer."

"Thanks! I'm glad we got to talk, Val!"

Mormons did not encourage serious dating until you finished your mission and were ready to get married. Before that time, dating life involved a lot of group dates to get to know as many people as possible before you settled down. I thought it was smart. Everything was still changing so much in high school; it made sense not to get attached to any one person before you knew what your life was going to be like. Of course, some people did get into serious relationships and wrote each other on their missions, but breaking the law of chastity was far up there on the scale of sins, seen in the same tier as murder in a sense, so it was best to stay away from that temptation.

Luckily, most of the local teenagers were Mormon. Gram told me my new school would have about a 75 percent Mormon population on campus, including teachers. She used to be a secretary there. I was glad I would be among people who understood my new lifestyle and values.

The Bittersweet Date Night: July 16, 1:37 AM

As I returned from my first date after moving to Arizona, I had a difficult realization. I had such an amazing time with Kirk and his friends, and it was cool to be the first girl he took out when he got home from his mission; however, part of me longs for that person who already knows and loves me, not one who has to learn about me. Also, there is no way it's going to work out with Kirk. It was just a fun date. Since he's home for his mission, he'll be encouraged to go find a girl and get married. It's part of the eternal plan.

On another note, it is hard wanting something you can't have. Part of me wants to go on a lot of group dates like everyone else and have a fun senior year of high school. It is a new adventure! Even though a fresh start is exciting, I long for the familiarity of truly knowing someone and who they are already. It is complicated when the one person your heart craves is 3,000 miles away and waking up for early-morning football practice right about now. I miss Jayce.

But the Lord's timing is perfect. He is so good. I know the prophets of the Church speak truth and speak of the true gospel. I'm not sure of His whole plan for me right now, but I have faith that it will be nothing less than wonderful. I may be sad about Jayce, but it will be all right.

Remember, God's timing is always perfect.

Signing off for now,

Val

The Stereotypical Future: July 30, 8:57 PM

The other week in church in Young Women, we talked about our role as a woman in the world. We can't have the priesthood authority that the Lord restored to the earth through Joseph Smith. I don't understand that, but we talked about what special plans the Lord has for women. It made me excited to have a family one day. I cannot wait to one day be married inside of the temple and have it last for all time and eternity. I cannot wait to teach my kids the way that Heavenly Father wants us to live and raise them in the Church and tell them my conversion story. I have been very independent my entire life so far and didn't want anything to do with being tied down, but it is all about perspective. I want nothing more than to at some point in my life be a mother and a wife. I want to be the best at both. It brings me comfort that I'll have something so perfect and eternal through the temple.

Signing off for now,

Val

School would begin in just a few days, and Gram and I had gone shopping for school clothes. That was fun. I talked to Mom and Dad, and they were doing good. Mom wished me luck for my baptism on Saturday and receiving the gift of the Holy Ghost on Sunday at church. I loved and missed them both a lot.

The Adventure Begins: August 5, 11:36 PM

Tomorrow is my first day at Summit Vista High as a senior. I feel intimidated and excited. My friends won't be waiting for me in the cafeteria or homeroom like in years past, but I'm looking forward to all the new opportunities.

The hardest part is that no one understands how truly difficult all of this is for me. Just because God's will be above mine doesn't make it any easier to follow. I try to remind myself that my challenge now only confirms that it will be worth it—at least that is a comforting feeling going into a new place being so uneasy. I know He has a reason for making everything so uncomfortable and lonely right now.

Big day tomorrow, signing off,

Val

Chapter Six

TAKING CHANCES

*"When you take risks, you learn that there will be times
when you succeed and there will be times when you fail,
and both are equally important."*
Ellen DeGeneres

SUMMER/AUTUMN

I RODE TO SCHOOL on the first day with a few of the girls from my Young Women group at church. We did not have any of the same classes or lunch periods, but at least I was not going to show up on the first day without anyone. I said goodbye to them and began to navigate the campus to my first class. Bells rang and student piled into the air-conditioned classrooms, a welcome break from the 100-plus-degree weather outside. For me, the classrooms did not feel like a break. I had never been so stressed in my life about going to school.

All the doors were closed, and I finally stumbled upon my first class, Senior Honors English. I opened the door as quietly as possible and turned to shut it. As I faced the class from the doorway, everyone stared. I felt embarrassed and caught off guard. At Mountain Valley, someone would have called my name and said hi or jumped up to give a hug after a long summer. This experience was the complete opposite.

The teacher kindly told me there was a seat for me in the front. This was not like church; I did not want to sit in the front here—I wanted to hide. She handed out assignment sheets and rules. When the bell rang at the end of class, I did not waste any time. Finding each class in time to claim the most hidden seat available was the only thing on my mind.

Three more classes went by, and in those I was barely noticed, or I did not care anymore. I knew a few people from church in my seminary class. Seminary occurred during a class period where kids could either take an elective or study the scriptures with teachers in a church building right across campus. Most of the Mormons did seminary. I felt a bit more at ease in that class. I was not used to being shy at all, so having a break to talk and socialize about similarities was nice. Also, most of the people in my class, including my teacher, knew about my baptism coming up. Gram knew just about everyone in town, and she was elated about having me in Arizona and my making the decision to be baptized—she could not hide it. I didn't blame her; I was excited, too.

"Good morning, Brothers and Sisters! It's nice to have you all here for another year of seminary. This year we are doing an intense study of the Old Testament of the Bible and connecting it back to the Book of Mormon as we move along. I'm extremely excited to get started with this! How was everyone's summer?" Brother Richards asked the class.

Most of the students hooted and hollered to show enthusiasm. We then moved on to a game that would help us get to know each other. It came to my turn. Brother Richards had introduced me as Sandy Parker's granddaughter from West Virginia and asked me to tell my story. When discussing testimony and conversion, many

Mormons tended not to be shy. I finally had a class where I could be the new me. I told the class where I was from, how I moved away from my family, how I was sick and lost, and how I decided to get a fresh start here in Arizona while getting the support needed to join the Church.

People were nice. When traveling back to campus, everyone told me they were glad I chose to come to Arizona, that I was brave, and that I had a strong testimony. I appreciated that.

After seminary was lunch. No one from seminary class had lunch at the same time as me, so I went to the library and found a quiet corner. I unpacked my sandwich, chips, apple, and Dr. Pepper as I scrolled through social media while eating in silence. I was not used to that either. I was not sure if I liked it or not.

I finished my classes for the day and met the girls from Young Women to ride home. I told them my day was good and that I liked campus. *They would not understand; there's no point in explaining what it was really like.* Tomorrow I was set to audition for the show choir at Summit Vista. If I made it in, I would need a schedule change, which I was honestly fine with. *I hope I make it. I could make more friends there.*

Thursday morning came, and my online schedule had changed before the school day began. *I made it in, yes!* I was excited to have another opportunity to make friends and be more comfortable here.

It turned out that most of the show choir kids ate in a large group every day, and one of them invited me to sit with them. *Finally something familiar.* I would not have to eat lunch completely alone anymore.

I went home that day with a bigger smile on my face than in days past. Gram was happy to see that. She had begun to worry about me. We had an after-school talk with snacks at the counter in the kitchen. In West Virginia, I used to just dart off to my room, rush to dance, and try to avoid my family, who always seemed to be pestering me. Gram and I ate fresh fruit while we talked about my schedule changes and how I did not really have any friends yet, but at least I had a group to be with. She asked how I liked seminary and told me that Brother Richards used to be a student at Summit Vista when she was a secretary there. He went to college and came back to teach seminary classes. She was glad I was starting to like things more.

We heard a gentle knock on the front door. I answered it, and there stood Mitch.

"Hey, Val! Remember me? From the other night at the pool at my parents' house?"

"Of course! Hi, Mitch! How are you?"

"I'm good! My mom told me it was your first week at Summit Vista High. I graduated last year, and I figured you may want to drive around and go to dinner? I could show you around."

I looked at Gram. She smiled and came to the door. She knew Mitch and was excited to see him. She hugged him and returned to the kitchen, leaving us to our conversation.

"Yeah, I think that would be really fun, actually. That's cool of you, Mitch!"

"Awesome! Well, let's say six tomorrow?"

"Sounds great. I'll see ya then!"

We said our goodbyes, and I closed the door. Gram was of course smiling. I grinned at her and went to my room to shower and get into comfortable clothes.

My baptism date was only two days away, and I knew how important it was for Church members to help others understand that they belonged in the true church with the rest of us—especially those who had fallen away. I was going to invite Mitch to my baptism, but I was not on a mission to convert him; I just enjoyed his friendship.

Friday at school came and went, and Mitch picked me up for our date.

"So, are you going to tell me where we're going, or am I going to be surprised?"

"I hate surprises, so I'll tell you mostly everything."

I laughed. I hated surprises too. "You already have the whole night planned?"

"Of course I do! You're cute and fun, and you deserve to have a good time and not worry."

"That is really cool. I don't think I've had a planned date before."

"Well, I'm glad I can experience that with you. Here's the plan I had in mind: I say we go to Los Favoritos Taco Shop. It's a hole-in-the-wall taco place, and it's the best."

"That sounds delicious! I love Mexican food. It's my favorite, but it's rare to find authentic Mexican food in West Virginia. Good thinking, Mitch."

We giggled.

"Then I thought we could stop by the Soda Shop. You take a soda and mix it with flavors. It's so good. And I know you don't drink coffee, so I thought soda might be a good pick-me-up. I never did understand that about the Church, but I respect that. Oh, and they have the best cookies there too. Lastly, I figured it would be fun to go to TopGolf."

"I've heard of that place!"

"I think you'll like it. It's like really cool mini golf, but inside and from a ledge!"

"You're good at this planning dates thing."

"Yeah, you get to be good at it, growing up here. Not that they ever became anything much, but when you are Mormon, you go on a lot of dates, and you have to keep things interesting. I never understood the concept of dating just for fun. I have always wanted to find someone I really like and keep that going, rather than stress about how many other people I could be dating. Simply weird to me."

"I agree. I don't know, I'm sure there's a reason for it, but I get where you're coming from."

We pulled up to the taco shop, and Mitch opened my door. After our delicious dinner, he turned to me with a smile. "I know I said I hate surprises, but I have to show you the Arizona sunset. Is that okay?"

"I love a good sunset, and I may not be a West Virginia fan, but I can tell you it would be hard to beat one of the sunsets coming over the Appalachian Mountains," I replied with a grin.

"Okay, we will see!"

We hopped into the car and drove to a nearby overlook. My breath was taken away. It might not have beat a West Virginia sunset, but I had to admit that this one was beautiful, vibrant, and simply different—a good different. Bright fire reds dimmed as the purples and pinks took over the sky that would soon be full of stars and city lights.

Dates never went like this in West Virginia. There was nothing to do there; here, it was a whole new and exciting world. And the night wasn't over yet.

The date proceeded as he said—with no worries. It was nice. We finished at the indoor golfing place, laughing and talking: about how and why I moved to Arizona, and about how he fell away from the Church—everything. It was so refreshing. Everything about this experience was refreshing. I loved every second of it.

Before the end of the night, on the ride home, I invited him to my baptism. He said yes, which made me happy. We said good night, and I ran inside to tell Gram everything that had happened.

A New Friend: August 9, 12:08 AM

   True happiness is found when you find a place and a person that you can be yourself with. I know that Heavenly Father is looking out for me and has always been saving me for an amazing guy who is perfect for me.

   Mitch is a wonderful, kindhearted gentleman. I couldn't have asked for a more enjoyable night. I'm going to like it here; it may not be so lonely.

   For now,

   Val

I woke up on the morning of my baptism, got into my white dress that I'd picked out specifically for today, and got ready. When people grew up in the Church, they got baptized when they were eight years old. Their parents gave them the choice to do so or not, and typically they said yes. In some cases, the child waited, or there was a later-in-life convert to the Church, and I was one of those who chose to be baptized after I learned the truth.

Everything went perfectly. I was baptized as a member of the Church of Jesus Christ of Latter-day Saints. I was thrilled, renewed, and ready to become a member of His true church. Afterward, we had food and lemonade to celebrate. The room was full for both the baptism and the celebration.

That week went well at school. I was in an elevated state of comfort. School at Summit Vista was nothing like Mountain Valley. I just went to class, enjoyed seminary and show choir, and then went home. A couple of weeks went by like that. Mitch and I continued to date and enjoy each other's friendship. We went on a lot of adventures and ate a lot of good tacos.

Focus on the Temple: August 29, 12:04 AM

So, Mitch and I went driving and on a date today. When crossing a red light we didn't see, we crashed. Mitch tried to avoid oncoming traffic, and in turning, we got pretty banged up and knocked an intersection to pieces when crossing into the median. Mitch's truck was totaled, but he made the smart decision and kept us alive. As we were forcing the truck to turn the way of traffic, I closed my eyes. As I looked up right after the wreck had happened, I saw the temple, Captain Moroni trumpeting toward the sky in all white and gold on its gigantic white pillars of stone. The temple is God's way of sealing in eternity. I love it, and I love that I can go into some sections now. It is my comfort and my peace. Thank you, Heavenly Father, for keeping Mitch and I alive today. I'll tell this story everywhere I go.

Thankful,

Val

What I Believe: September 1, 3:27 PM

I believe in destiny and the plan of a loving Heavenly Father. I believe and I know that this church is true. When I moved across the country, following the plan God had for me, I had no idea it would be so wonderful. I didn't realize the depth of the trials, magical moments, adventures, friendships, and laughter I would have after only a few months of living somewhere completely new. How different life would be if I didn't follow that plan. It is crazy to think about.

Until later,

Val

Ugh, So Many Thoughts: September 13, 11:07 PM

I broke up with Mitch tonight. Shocker, I know. I cried a lot, but it needed to be done. The last few days were tough for us. He wanted to see me all the time, but I had a lot of schoolwork to do. I feel as if most people would be understanding toward that. He was not, which worried me into thinking this was moving too fast, and he was too attached. He became controlling, and I didn't want that.

I'm glad he started going back to church and seems to be gaining a testimony again. He said he may even go on a mission. Our relationship was not long, and I think I'll have a friend in him once things calm down, but for now we need our distance. All of this caused me to reflect on who I am without a boy.

I'm Val Beckley, the one who moved across the country to chase the true church in one of its most supportive environments. I love the outdoors, peaceful things, and busy schedules. I'm free-spirited, but I'll always choose the path of God. I love this gospel and all the blessings that I'm unable to give proper thanks for. Unfortunately, I still live each day with a bit more anxiety than I hope for, but I know that if I follow the prophet and his council, I can be calmer and know it will be fine. I'm so grateful that everything happens for a reason. I'm grateful to be me, without a boy.

Signing off,

Val

After Mitch and I broke up, Gram and I went into the temple. She said it might help me sort things out in my head. I had been to the temple once since my baptism, but my excitement during my first experience overwhelmed me, and I did not focus much on the calmness the environment could lend.

We dressed in our skirts, brought our scriptures, and parked at the entranceway to the Mesa Arizona Temple. It was a beautiful tropical-island getaway in the middle of a dry desert. Palm trees, floral arrangements in gardens, fresh grass, waterfalls, and reflection pools lined the grounds of the magnificent white building. We walked in, showed our temple recommends to the priesthood holder, and entered, feeling honored to do so. We changed into the white jumpsuits members wore to do baptisms for the dead. *Imagine explaining that to a family who thinks you joined a dangerous cult.*

There were no literal dead people being baptized. In short, baptisms for the dead in the temple acted to give each person who had died without having the opportunity to know the Church a chance to accept the true gospel. I liked performing these. It was peaceful to be in the temple, but it was also powerful to feel someone accept the gospel on the other side—especially if they were in your own family. Members of the Church were really into family history for many reasons, this being one of them.

Doing baptisms for the dead in the temple made me want more than ever for everyone I loved to find this truth while they were on earth, as I had been blessed to do. Mom might come around, and if I stuck to my faith that God would show them the way, my whole family could be together for eternity.

I would be lying if I said that the doctrine did not give me difficulties. If my family never made the decision to join the Church here or in the afterlife, I would not be with them in the kingdom of God. It broke my heart, but it made me want them to find the truth even more. *One day. I know they will find it one day. God would not have brought me all this way to not have my family with me in the end.* I told myself that often.

Purpose Driven: September 20, 12:20 AM
    Tonight, I was grateful to receive my patriarchal blessing. It is hard to explain such

a wonderful experience. You turn in a letter saying that you are ready to receive your blessing. The stake patriarch has you and your family over to his home, and they talk about your testimony. I got to bear my testimony of the gospel. After that, the patriarch gives you a special blessing and road map for your life, straight from Heavenly Father. I was told I was going to have a family and serve a mission. I'm so blessed to have received my patriarchal blessing. I know it came from Heavenly Father. He has a plan for me if I can continue to live a righteous life. I'm grateful for this gospel.

This is a post to promise myself that I'll serve an eighteen-month mission. That is what I want to do more than anything in life right now. I love that I can be a force for good and lead someone to the gospel, just like the missionaries did with me. I can tell people how they can be sealed to their families forever. I'll turn in my papers, and the Lord will tell me where He needs me through our living prophet, President Thomas S. Monson. I know that Heavenly Father restored His true church to the earth through the prophet Joseph Smith. I know that the Book of Mormon is true, and I'm grateful for its teachings of the fullness of the gospel.

Signing off hopeful,

Val

Creating Your Own Joy: October 2, 9:48 AM

Being away from everything I have ever known——my friends, family, life itself——I'm finding it hard to discover people who make me feel like it will all be okay in the long term. Sure, people are nice and kind, but they aren't best friends forever. It is hard to imagine that life is better here than it would be in West Virginia at this point. Mostly, yes, it is. But the longing for home I'm feeling isn't satisfied. I want to be at homecoming with my friends, not strangers I just met this summer. Everyone has their way of doing things. It is their senior year, too. I don't blame them. I just wish I could bring the familiarity of WV to my new school. Fall break is coming up. I may visit home. I don't have anything thing else to do, and it is okay that I miss it. Sometimes you just have to create your own joy. Just a bit lonely tonight.

Until later,

Val

I called Mom that night. The rest of my family was still bitter, but I really missed her. Dad was a bit more closed off, but I missed him too.

"Mom, what do you think about me coming back in a few weekends? We have an October break here, and I want to go to homecoming. I miss my friends, and plus, I cannot really go alone to Summit Vista's homecoming dance."

"Yeah, I understand that. It would be nice to see you! How about we split the price? Are you able to do that?" I had gotten a small editing and tutoring job at Summit Vista before and after school. I was paid to edit papers, tutor in English, and help in the library. The Parkers also provided me with so much, so I was able to save that money I earned from my job.

Mom and I made it happen, and I flew home for a visit in late October.

Chapter Seven

STUBBORN IN THE WAYS OF THE LORD

"Sometimes, we are our own worst enemies. One must learn to be discerning with one's own thoughts. We must be able to decipher the truth versus the lies in our minds. Otherwise, we become enslaved to the shackles of struggles we place on our own ankles."
Brittainy C. Cherry

AUTUMN

I WOKE UP in my old bed at Nan and Gramps' house. It felt good to be there, but also it felt awkward. I knew they felt negatively toward what I had done and how things had ended, so I simply embraced the fact that I had to walk on eggshells.

Tonight was homecoming. Mia had come over last night when I got to town from the airport and stayed with me at Nan and Gramps'. We played games and watched TV, eventually falling asleep. She was going to homecoming too, so we could get ready together.

When I rolled over, she was still sleeping in the twin bed next to me, so I did my routine as silently as possible. I unplugged my phone, read my scriptures, and prayed before beginning my day. I peeked outside at the leaves swiftly changing on the trees surrounding the house. It was October, but sometimes the temperatures shifted from winter-like mornings to humid summer days when we were in season transition. I had missed this. Arizona had seasons too, but not autumn. Autumn was always my favorite.

I enjoyed the view, put away my scriptures, and continued to unpack and get ready for the morning. I quietly unzipped my suitcase. I could hear Nan and Gramps moving around. You could hear everything in this house. They were up and ready to tackle the day, but I did not want to go out to the kitchen alone and get into small talk.

My suitcase was always too full, and this trip was no different. I took out my homecoming dress first, wrapped and ready to be hung on the door hook. Its lacey pink details with gems at the high waist, capped sleeves, and high neckline made for a comfortable, modest, yet fun look. I smiled as I hung it up. I took out my boots, sandals, slippers, and running shoes. Then I panicked. I had forgotten my homecoming shoes.

One of a high school girl's worst nightmares: anything going wrong for what would be one of her last school dances ever. I was already going alone, which I was fine with since I was visiting. *But to forget the perfect pair of shoes all the way across the country? Great.*

Mia woke up. I guess she had been disturbed by my huffing, puffing, and scrambling. She giggled.

"What is so funny?"

"Hey, hey, take it easy. I know you don't have your coffee anymore, but don't be a rude ass to me. I see you forgot something."

I laughed at her. I hated to admit it, but she was funny despite her vulgar language.

"I forgot my shoes, Mia. They were perfect. You should have seen them," I said mournfully.

"I'm sure they were awesome, Val, but they're about 3,000 miles away and impossible to get before tonight, so what's your plan? You've got to have one; you always do."

"Well, I have to get to the mall. That's about all I know."

Mia was not old enough to drive yet, and everyone else had commitments, jobs, or duties to fulfill today. No one was available until right before homecoming when we planned pictures on Nan and Gramps' porch. The two of them had left for work while I was discovering my mistake.

The house was silent. Mia winked at me, making me feel like she was up to no good. She pointed in the direction of Jayce's house and grinned. *Oh dear, she is truly up to no good.*

"Call Jayce. He got that old Chevy Nova working with his dad, and I'm sure he would love to take you to the mall in that beautiful car. But he must take me with you, because if I'm being honest, I love the car, and I forgot a pair of shoes too."

We both laughed. Mia and I were so different, but despite my best and obsessive planning efforts and Mia's love for having things fall into place, we both forgot shoes. And Mia had the right idea. Jayce was the only one of my friends who had a car and the only one who would be willing to take me this early in the morning to the mall of all places.

The phone rang a few times, and his sleepy voice answered.

"Val? What's up?"

"Hey, Jayce, how are you?"

"Tired, but good," he chuckled. "You?"

"I'm okay. Hey, I know it's been a few months since we've talked, but I kind of need a favor."

"You need a favor? In Arizona?"

"Oh, I thought you knew I was here. I'm visiting for homecoming weekend."

"That's awesome! Glad you're here for a bit. Anyway, whatcha need?"

"Well, long story short—"

"A short story! With you?! Yeah right, Val. You're the most complicated girl I know."

We laughed awkwardly. "I'm not! Anyway, I need you to take me to the mall if you have time today. I forgot my shoes for homecoming in my closet in Arizona."

He laughed, hard. *Rude.* "Of course I'll take you, Val. Give me twenty minutes and I'll be there. I need to get an outfit to match my date tonight anyway." He did not sound thrilled, but he always showed up. No matter what. He was the calm to my crazy.

"Oh, okay! Well, I'll see you in twenty minutes then. Oh, Mia needs a ride too. Can she sit in the back?"

"She will have to deal with the stink of wrestling stuff, but of course she can tag along. We'll grab breakfast, too."

"See you soon, Jayce!"

"See you soon, Val, and hey, it's nice to have you back for a few days."

My heart pounded. *Ugh.* We hung up, and I told Mia to throw on some clothes.

Jayce and his beauty of a car came rolling down the driveway exactly twenty minutes later. He was not on time much, but he was today. He was unpredictable and wonderful.

"Hey, guys, want to stop for breakfast at Kitty's Diner? My treat. I'm starving," Jayce explained. Mia and I agreed. It was not a hard sell. Kitty's was delicious, and I hadn't had Southern-style comfort food in a while and craved it.

Mia sat in the back like a good younger sister, preoccupied texting her friends about homecoming later. Jayce and I both turned toward each other at the same time. We smiled, and he spoke.

"So, are you going to the dance with all of your girlfriends?"

"Totally. Who are you going with? You sure did wait until the last minute. Would you have even gone to get an outfit if I didn't beg you to take me to the mall?"

"I'm supposed to go with Ashley Vinn. We've been getting to know each other. I just don't know. And I don't know if I would have gotten an outfit. I probably wouldn't have because who cares that much really?"

We laughed because clearly Mia and I did.

I did not recognize Jayce's tone when he mentioned Ashley Vinn. I let it go. She was nice, and I was sure they would look great together if he managed to match her. We turned on some music, and the tension drifted away.

After our breakfast at Kitty's, we arrived at the mall.

"Okay, Jayce, so what is Ashley wearing? You need to match her at least a little bit."

Mia went on her way to find shoes for her dress and keep a lookout for ones that would go well with mine while I helped Jayce.

"When we talked last, she said she's wearing red."

"What shade?"

"Don't really know, and I don't really care."

"Goodness. All right, then, we'll go with burgundy. That should look good with whatever shade she's got."

We went to a couple of stores and found Jayce a burgundy tie, suspenders, and socks to go with his black pants, white shirt, and shoes. He would look sharp.

Next on the agenda was to meet Mia at the shoe store. She should have a few pairs picked out for me to try on by now, which was good because we only had about five hours left, and we still needed to drive home and get ready for the night. I trusted her taste, so I wasn't worried.

On our walk to the store, Jayce spoke up about how he was feeling about homecoming.

"Honestly, Val, I don't want to go."

"You don't want to go to your senior homecoming?"

"No, it's not that. I just don't really want to go with her."

I was quiet for a moment. "Well, what do you want to do?"

He just looked at me while I looked back. I knew what he was thinking, but I was not going to be his backup date; I did not want to do that to Ashley. She was not my friend, but I could see how that would hurt a girl—to be abandoned by your date only for him to go with another girl who happened to come into town for the weekend.

"Well, Jayce, that's honestly up to you. You should have a fun last homecoming, so do whatever you want. It's only pictures and dinner."

"Yeah, but I don't even want to do those things with her."

"No offense, but why are you leading her on, then?"

He looked down, and then away.

Mia waved enthusiastically from the shoe store window and approached with one pair of shoes, not three like I thought she would have.

"Val, I found these and think they'll look amazing."

The shoes were gorgeous. A unique pair of closed-toed, petite chunky heels with a pointed toe. The color of the shoe was a strong nude with a hint of pink. The main embellishment on the shoe matched the middle of my dress and had burgundy stones throughout the design that I loved. Googly eyed, Mia and I both stared at the shoes while I tried them on. They were comfortable and a perfect fit. I felt so lucky.

I bought the shoes, everyone had what they needed for the dance, and we drove home—windows down in the Nova with the autumn breeze welcoming itself in. None of us minded.

The engine settled as we pulled into the driveway. I stayed in the car while Mia went inside to turn on the curling irons.

"So, did you decide what you're going to do about Ashley?"

"Yeah, I can't keep leading her on. Taking her to the dance would be misleading. I don't like her that much, but she's a friend."

"Okay, well, will I still see you at the dance then?"

"Would you like to maybe come to dinner with me? And then we can drive the Nova there together. It's up to you; I don't want to ruin any plans you had."

"Believe it or not, this time I don't have any plans. I just missed home and wanted to go to homecoming. And to answer your question, yes, I would love to do that."

"What time should I pick you up?"

"Let's say five to be safe."

"I'll see you then! You aren't upset that we won't match?"

"We are going to match! My shoes, remember?"

"Gotta love the shoes." He winked and drove off after I closed the door. As he turned the corner, he smiled and I smiled back.

Mia and I had the house to ourselves until it was time for pictures. We blasted music, got ready, and ate snacks. It felt good to be with my little sister again. She was growing up a lot, and while I felt the disconnect between us, I loved her and wanted her to be a part of the world I had found in Arizona. It would happen in time, I was sure. For that moment, though, we just got ready for homecoming together, her first and my last.

When I told her about what Jayce had said to me in the car, she laughed a deep belly laugh.

"I knew it! You came in glowing too much for that not to have happened, Val."

"Oh, Mia, stop that! Of course I'm thrilled to be going with him, but I'm leaving in two days, and I need to remember that. I have school to finish and a mission to go on."

"Please at least kiss the guy."

"Mia! You are something else." We laughed together, and she did that winking thing again as if to say, "Who do you think you're fooling?"

We finished getting ready, and before we knew it, it was time for friends to start arriving for pictures. Jayce came right at the end, and we took a few photos together as well. Dad was the main photographer, but everyone was there—Nan, Gramps, Renee, Sarah and her friends, John, Mom, and Paul. It went by quickly, and then we all tended to our dinner plans.

Jayce and I took off in the Nova, but not before Dad could shake his hand and tell us he hoped we would have a wonderful time. Not the typical response from a dad, but he knew I was flying back to Arizona in a few days, leaving us both heartbroken. I am sure he was hoping that Jayce would sweep me off my feet so that I would never go back to Arizona to live with the Parkers. That was not going to happen, but I was excited to be going with Jayce.

Chapter Eight

HOMECOMING AND HOME LEAVING

*"We leave something of ourselves behind when we leave a place,
we stay there, even though we go away. And there are things
in us that we can find again only by going back there."*
Pascal Mercier

AUTUMN

HOMECOMING: THE TIME when the school came together to celebrate the year, the school, and what the school had taught them as their alma mater. It was also a time to dance in a sweaty gym near your dearest friends and get drunk later. I was only going to be doing one of those things, and I was perfectly fine with that.

Jayce and I pulled up, and in the time it took Jayce to get my door, at least three football friends with their dates came up to greet him. Thomas was the one who ended up at my door first, opening it for me. I loved his sweet soul.

"Val, you are one of the cutest girls here. How is Jayce going to let you just stay in the car?"

"Thomas! You are too kind," I said as I got out to hug him. It had been months. "To be fair, he was only out of the car for one second before being attacked with love from y'all."

Thomas giggled and took my arm to walk me to Jayce. Everyone stared. They stared because we looked like we had planned this all along, and everyone knew that Jayce had been getting to know Ashley. Despite the stares, I also received several looks of approval. That made me straighten my back and walk a little more confidently.

"I get to bring the Western girl to homecoming," Jayce said to his friends with a grin.

"Yeah, you're Jayce's Western girl," Thomas remarked. I missed Thomas quite a bit, and I was pleased to see him. Despite that, I gave him the most loving glare one could give. I was not Jayce's, but I was now known as the Western girl. *Cool.*

Thomas and Jayce hung back for a while, quietly talking. We all met up to walk in. I hugged some of my favorite teachers who were there supervising, then my friends, and then Mia, Sarah, and John, who had shown up already.

Jayce and I went our separate ways for the faster dances as he was not much of a dancer. I liked that I did not have to impress anyone; I just danced. He made sure to find me during the slow dances, though. He knew that mattered. We shared many sweet dances together that night, pulling my heart and my head into a trap of imagining what it would be like if I did stay. Jayce could tell I was deep in thought, and he did not say a word. *Ugh. Why does he have to be here and so far away?*

It was the last song of the night, according to the DJ, and Charlie Puth was singing about catching up with a friend when they saw each other again. We swayed and talked.

"Come with me to Arizona. Or at least after we graduate."

Jayce looked stunned. "Val, why can't you just come back home? I think you're being stubborn."

"Because, Jayce, there are barely any Mormons here. That is my life now. I know you think it's silly, but it is the truth, and I know it. It's such a different environment."

"Yeah, you've told me. You do know it's cult, right?"

I glared at him, a less loving glare than Thomas received earlier. Jayce was comfortable here, and that was great for him, but not for me. "No, it is not."

We ended the conversation awkwardly and bluntly. He could not see the bigger picture. He only saw senior year, graduating, and staying in West Virginia. I had seen so much more since I moved out West.

My thought ended with the song and the end of the homecoming dance. Jayce and I were not fighting, but I think we both truly knew it was not going to work out with us now.

He took me back home to Nan and Gramps', and we sat in the Nova for a while and talked some more. Tomorrow was my last day in West Virginia for a while. I was scheduled to leave on Monday morning, and tomorrow I was going to visit family before I headed back. This was my night to say goodbye to Jayce again. We talked, laughed, and I cried because I would miss him. It was nearly 2 a.m., and it was time to say good night.

"Jayce, I'm going to miss you. I hope you know that."

"You wouldn't have to if you'd just stay, you know? Life isn't as hard and complicated as you make it out to be, Val."

"I know, but I need to follow the Lord's plan for me in Arizona. Everything happens for a reason."

"I don't get that."

"Yeah, sometimes I don't understand it either, but I know it's right. I also know that nothing worth having comes easy."

"I guess." There was a pause and a sense of heartbreak in that old Chevy Nova, surrounded by the chill of a cold October night. "I'm going to miss you too, Val."

He reached over, touched my thigh, looked me in the eyes and hugged me. I hugged him back, harder than I had ever hugged him before. It was a long hug that I never wanted to end. A tear fell from his face. He knew this time it would be goodbye for the long haul.

Neither of us wanted the night to end.

He grabbed my tear-stained face, moved my hair out of the way, and glanced down at my blush-and-burgundy-colored shoes we had searched for that morning. He smiled softly, looked at me again, and then time stood still.

Jayce Adams and I kissed for several minutes that night—sad, long, and desperate kisses filled with love from all the years that we had never kissed before. He moved his hand further up my thigh with each minute that passed. I gently moved his hand back down to my knee and kissed him one last time. It was heartbreaking and magical. I loved him, and it was time for me to leave the boy that loved me back, yet again.

Jayce drove home, and I finished my weekend with my family in West Virginia and was on a flight back to Phoenix before I knew it. I felt a little guilty about what had happened in the car, but I knew the Lord would forgive me if I asked him to.

SPRING

I missed everyone in West Virginia during the lonely parts of the night, especially Jayce, but I was at peace in my little corner of the world again. There was less temptation here, and I focused on finishing school and preparing for a worthy mission as a servant of the Lord and His church.

The winter months flew by, and graduation was finally around the corner. Mom, Dad, and Renee were coming to see me walk across stage to get my diploma. They would sit with the Parker family. They all seemed to get along now. I think they realized that I had made my choice and was doing what I felt best for my life.

I had many friends but no close friends. Mitch and his family were all serving missions and were in a different district now. The Church was constantly growing, and boundaries had to be redrawn.

Aside from show choir and working in the student library, I spent my free time reading the scriptures, working on homework, and thinking of what life would be like when I was on my mission. I was almost ready to turn in my papers so that the prophet and apostles could pray over where the Lord needed me most. When I graduated, I would send them to Salt Lake City.

Every day, people told me that my conversion story would profoundly move others to decide to follow the truth of the gospel of Jesus Christ. I was ready to preach the gospel that had changed my life so dramatically.

Once graduation rolled around, I did not feel that sadness that many felt as they got ready to leave their precious school, friends, and memories. I felt not the least bit nostalgic toward the memories and friends I had made in Arizona, but this was only part of my journey. If anything, I would miss Arizona sunsets, the Parker family, and my own family when I became a missionary for eighteen months.

I got to show Mom, Dad, and Renee where I had been spending my time. I took them to the taco shop, my church, school, the soda joint, my favorite sunset-watching spots, and where I lived with the Parkers. Mom was happy to see the Parker family again, and Dad and Renee were civil and kind.

I graduated, and that was that. It was a quick moment in time compared to what was in store.

While I was leaving the arena that housed all the graduates, trying to find those who came to see me, I overheard a conversation between two boys from the Young Men group at church who had also graduated that day. Harper Mason and Bryce Rinehart were discussing where they were being called on their missions.

"I got called to Guam. I am so pumped! Bishop Reed said I was worthy, and I can't wait to be there!" Bryce said.

"That's sick, bro. I got mine yesterday to go to California in a couple of weeks!" Harper responded. "Bishop didn't care about you and Christina?"

"I mean, I told him mostly everything. I said that I had repented for touching her, so I guess it's cool. I mean, I have my mission call, so it's fine," Bryce said.

"Totally. That's awesome, dude. You'll be a great missionary."

I thought of how exciting it must be to get your mission call.

A couple of days later, once my family had left Arizona and summer began, I set up a meeting with my bishop, Bishop Reed, to turn in my mission papers. It was a serious meeting.

I dressed in church clothes, per the usual for meetings and any church event that was not casual. Skirt, nice blouse, and scripture bag. Bishop Reed was a kind man, so I did not have jitters or nervousness when going to talk with him. Gram came with me, but she would sit outside and wait, and then we'd get tacos to celebrate.

"Are you nervous at all?"

"No, not really. Bishop Reed is great, and I feel good about the interview."

"That's great, sweetie. You will make the best missionary. I'm thrilled for you. You are going to change lives. Your story is powerful."

"I sure hope so!"

The bishop opened his office door. "Hello, Sister Beckley!"

"Hi, Bishop Reed! How are you today?"

"I'm well. Thank you for asking. What about you, Sister Parker? How are you?"

"I'm good. I love having Val around. We have had a wonderful year."

"That is great news. Let's get this meeting started! We have a great missionary to send off!"

I entered his office and sat for a prayer. Meetings always began with a prayer.

"Dearest Father in Heaven, Sister Beckley and I sit here today to determine her worthiness to become a full-time missionary on Your errand. May we be honest, guided, and kind toward each other as we continue with this interview and meeting about her moving forward in missionary service. May our light guide, inspire, and teach us. We are grateful for your gospel, for what it teaches, and how it leads us in this life. We are grateful for the Savior, and for His sacrifice for us. We love you, Father, and we ask all of these things in the name of Your son, Jesus Christ, amen."

We ended the prayer, and I felt calm. Bishop Reed gave good prayers. I loved everything about the Church, and I was thrilled to teach the gospel soon, if this interview went well. The kiss between Jayce and I passed through my mind.

"Okay, Sister Beckley, tell me more about why you want to serve a mission."

"I want to be a missionary because I know it is something the Lord wants me to do. I know there are people out there who are just like I was: lost, confused, and looking for answers. Because of the missionaries here in Arizona, I was able to find the true church. I'm full of joy to know the truth, and I can't wait to share that with others who haven't found it yet. I also am excited to travel, meet new members of the Church, and grow as a member myself."

"That's great. Tell me what some of your concerns are while serving as a full-time missionary."

"I think my biggest concerns while serving a mission are missing my family and friends, not giving up when it gets hard, and meeting standards and expectations."

"You will be a wonderful missionary. Do you pray, ask for answers, and read the Book of Mormon every single day?"

"Yes, I do."

"Do you believe in the modern revelation that Joseph Smith restored to the earth, meaning that he was the prophet of the restoration of the gospel and that Thomas S. Monson is currently the called prophet of God?"

"Absolutely."

"Now, Sister Beckley. Missionaries live at a higher standard, as they must remain worthy to teach but also to set a selfless example. Do you pay a full tithe?"

"Yes, I do. Whenever I'm employed and have the means to do so."

"Do you attend church, take the sacrament worthily, and attend events each week?"

"Yes, I do."

"Do you attend the temple on a weekly basis?"

"I do now; it is one of my favorite places to be."

These were all questions bishops everywhere asked to decide worthiness and faithfulness.

"Have you committed any serious sin that you feel that you need to repent for, including but not limited to stealing, lying, participating in homosexual behavior, or breaking the law of chastity?"

I thought of the moment between Jayce and I months ago. I knew I had been forgiven, but I felt the need to say something.

"Honestly, Bishop, in October I visited home. There was this boy that I have known for a long time. We kissed and he touched me a little bit above the knee."

"Oh, well, Sister Beckley, how far did he touch you? The Lord takes the law of chastity extremely seriously since the law is in place for the safeguarding of procreation among his children. How far above the knee did he touch?"

"I understand that. I felt bad about what happened, but it was only a kiss that went just a little too far, and I stopped it."

"Kissing is fine, Sister, but when you experience anything sexual such as the young man holding your thigh and especially higher and touching your private parts to arouse those feelings, you lose the Holy Spirit, and you are tempted into sinful behavior. What did you feel when the young man touched you?"

"I'm not too sure, but I did stop it," I said, looking at the ground. That was the first time I had been touched like that, and I knew how I felt, but I also knew it made me unworthy.

"Sister Beckley, you did the right thing by not letting this go any further. The Lord is grateful that you know how important the law of chastity is, and I think it would be important for you to take a month to think about what happened and how it could have ended poorly. I think if you take the time to repent, pray to the Lord for full forgiveness, and remain worthy, you will be ready to turn in your mission paperwork in about a month," he concluded.

My heart crashed as Bishop Reed ended our meeting. Gram and I still went out for tacos afterward. She was always so positive, loving, and encouraging. She made me feel better about what had happened. There was no discussion about it once I told her the decision. She just told me, "The Lord's timing is perfect."

I knew that to be true for so many reasons; however, I did question Bishop Reed's decision that I would need to wait to serve a mission, while the young man I had overheard did not. *He didn't seem sorry for what he did. I liked kissing Jayce, yes, but I stopped it when I personally felt like it had gone too far for my beliefs and my values. Why couldn't I just repent personally and figure that out between me and God? And why was my transgression worse than that of the guy I overheard the other day at graduation?*

The bitterness soon faded into determination to make the month fly by and receive full forgiveness from the Lord. I knew He had already forgiven me, but it was important to prove that I had a newfound dedication to being obedient, which was one of the most important qualities in a missionary, according to the preparation guides I had read.

Chapter Nine

A NEW JOURNEY

"For what it's worth: it's never too
late to be whoever you want to be."
F. Scott Fitzgerald

SUMMER

AFTER WAITING A MONTH to turn in my papers for missionary service, I finally sent them along for consideration on placement.

The follow-up meeting with Bishop Reed went well, and he gave a prayer that encouraged me to move forward into the position of being a full-time missionary with the support of the Church. Along with members of a council, Bishop Reed said that the Lord wanted me to serve a mission without worrying about finances or emotional support.

"Sister Beckley, I know Heavenly Father is pleased with your heartfelt dedication, honesty, and passion toward His gospel. We, as a ward, have felt moved to send you on your mission fully paid if you would accept. Either way, we can send in your paperwork and wait to find out where you are called to preach the gospel. You have a powerful and relatable story about your conversion to the gospel, and we think it will bless many lives to see the truth."

I was speechless. I forgot about everything that had happened, all the anger and confusion, and knew it all was worth it.

Another New Adventure Ahead: July 25, 2:03 AM

    I haven't recorded my life here for a while, but today was a wonderful day that I feel should be documented. After a full repentance process, becoming more dedicated to the Church, and meeting with Bishop Reed, I was finally able to send in my papers for a mission. They should be returned to me within two weeks, and I'll know where the Lord has called me to serve and share the gospel. On top of all that good news, Bishop Reed proceeded to tell me that the Church wanted to pay for me to serve. I am the only member in my family, which they knew, and they want me to focus on sharing my story and becoming the best member I can be while serving for eighteen months.

    I feel blessed. I know Heavenly Father hears our prayers, wants us to succeed, and blesses us when we are obedient to Him. This will be a long two weeks of waiting, but I'm at peace, knowing what is ahead will be nothing less than fantastic! I was baptized a year ago. What a fantastic way to celebrate. I hope my family sees my decision to serve and considers why I'm doing it. I know they will find the truth one day.

    Hopeful,

    Val

The mail carrier arrived at our home early the day my mission call finally came. In her busy hands she held the decision that the prophets of God had made when praying about where I was needed as a missionary. I looked out the window as she opened the mailbox, placing inside the giant white envelope, which read *The Church of Jesus Christ of Latter-day Saints*. After retrieving the envelope, I sprinted back inside with the biggest smile I'd had in a long time.

A lot of members held small parties to celebrate the new missionary. As they opened the letter for the first time, everyone gathered around in anticipation. There were usually tears, screams, and hugs. It was a big event. This was exciting, but it also meant I had to wait until the weekend for the big reveal. *The ultimate torture: waiting, while the envelope looks you in the eyes every day from your dresser.*

Called to Serve: August 10, 4:23 PM

I'm in my room, about a half hour before I get to open the envelope!! People are starting to arrive and get seats. I managed to sneak away for a moment to write about how excited I am for this moment. I feel like after tonight, once I know where I'm going, everything will change and be so fast paced. I just want to take a moment and slow down. I'm so grateful for this gospel and for where it has taken me. I can't wait to tell people the good news. I have no idea what to expect, but I'm ready to learn, be obedient, and serve selflessly.

The living room is getting louder. I'm so nervous. I better go out there and start saying hello to everyone. Before I know it, it will be five, and I'll be ripping that envelope open. Let's do this!

Full of butterflies,

Val

Gram had already begun a FaceTime with Mom, and I was dialing for Dad so they could both watch. The entire living room was full of friends, church members, and leaders. Gram ran off to grab the envelope. She had hidden it so that I would not be tempted to open it. It was five o'clock, and with smiles on everyone's faces, I opened the letter. For five minutes, time stood still, and I heard nothing but silence as I read aloud to the crowd.

Dear Sister Beckley,

You are hereby called to serve as a missionary of the Church of Jesus Christ of Latter-day Saints. You are assigned to labor in the Texas Fort Worth Mission. It is anticipated that you will serve for a period of eighteen months.

I stopped, cried for a moment, and continued to read, barely hearing the echo of excitement in the background.

You should report to the Missionary Training Center on August 31, 2016. You will prepare to preach the gospel in the English language. Your assignment may be modified according to the needs of the mission president.

You have been recommended as one worthy to represent the Lord as a minister of the restored gospel. You will be an official representative of the Church. As such, you will be expected to maintain the highest standards of conduct and appearance by keeping the commandments, living mission rules, and following the council of your mission president. As you devote your time and attention to serving the Lord, leaving behind all other personal affairs, the Lord will bless you with increased knowledge and testimony of the Restoration and the truths of the gospel of Jesus Christ.

Your purpose will be to invite others to come unto Christ by helping them receive the restored gospel through faith in Jesus Christ and His Atonement, repentance, baptism, receiving the gift of the Holy Ghost, and enduring to the end. As you serve with all your heart, might, and strength, the Lord will lead you to those who are prepared to be baptized.

The Lord will reward you for the goodness of your life. Greater blessings and more happiness than you have yet experienced await you as you humbly and prayerfully serve the Lord in this labor of love among His children. We place in you our confidence and pray that the Lord will help you become an effective missionary.

You will be set apart as a missionary by your stake president. Please send your written acceptance promptly, endorsed by your bishop.

Please read the enclosed papers to better help you and your family prepare for your upcoming service.

Sincerely,

Thomas S. Monson, President

I was headed to Texas in only a few short weeks. Elated did not come close to describing how thrilled I was to be called to the Lone Star State. This would be a challenge, but one I was ready for. The Lord had prepared me. I had a lot of work to do, but I was eager to get started and share my story of coming to the truth.

END OF AUTUMN

Here Goes Nothin': August 29, 10:29 AM

The last few weeks have been terribly busy. I haven't had much time to write. Every morning I wake up and begin what will soon be my daily routine. I immediately pray, study the scriptures a little bit, and then exercise. My asthma has been acting up lately in this Arizona heat, but I have been pushing through. My body needs to be strong and prepared for the humidity of Texas. Of course, Arizona has prepared me for the heat just fine. After working out, I make myself and Gram (sometimes Mr. Parker when he isn't fishing) a fresh breakfast before we begin the day. While Gram gets ready, I usually study the Book of Mormon or read past General Conference talks. Bishop Reed has counseled me to stay focused, prepared, and eager.

I get set apart as a missionary tomorrow night and go through the temple tonight, so today and tomorrow are the days I have left to get everything together. As soon as Gram is ready for the day, we will go get what's left on the list: plenty of below-the-knee skirts, a temple dress and bag, temple garments, and comfortable shoes.

Gram started to explain temple garments to me yesterday afternoon, but she said that most of the information is what I'll be learning in the temple tonight. She said they are worn all the time for modesty purposes, but also as a daily reminder of our love and covenant relationship with God. I was told to focus, pray, and prepare spiritually before going tonight. This is a big decision. You must be endowed in the temple to go on a mission, and to eventually be eternally with Heavenly Father. It is an essential and humbling step.

Gram also told me not to stress about everything in the temple—that I get to go back as many times as I want in order to understand, but for tonight to just focus on how I feel when I'm getting my endowment. I'm glad she will be there with me. Bishop Reed, the stake president, a few of the Young Women leaders, the missionaries, and the entire Parker family will be going as well.

Gram made sure I knew that there were two parts to the endowment ceremony.

She said the first part I should expect is a private portion, and that is when I'll be able to wear the temple garments officially. She said that the second part is a movie, and it's with everyone in the session as a group setting. She said I'll learn a lot about the plan of salvation and how all people can return to the presence of the Lord. She said that after the whole ceremony, I'll be able to sit in the most beautiful room while I pray, study the scriptures, and discuss the experience; since it is a sacred experience, it is important not to talk about it outside of the temple. She said it is indescribable and I'll love it. I'm sure I will. I love this gospel and can't wait to make deeper promises with God.

Until afterward,

Val

Following the ceremony, I felt the most peace I had ever felt in my life thus far. None of it was controversial to me. All my prayers had been answered. I felt blessed to have had received this knowledge and make promises with God, and I wanted everyone in the Fort Worth, Texas, area to know the same. I was ready to preach the gospel as the Lord's servant and as a member of the Church of Jesus Christ of Latter-day Saints.

After I was set apart as a missionary and arrived at the missionary training center in Utah, the missionary service began. I checked in and went to my assigned location on the property, where I was allowed to send an email to my family, letting them know I was safe and what was happening.

Subject: Hello from the MTC!

Hi everyone! I just arrived at the MTC and wanted to let you all know I got here safely!

I can't draft a super-long email, but I wanted to share a few things:

I have heard "Welcome to the MTC" about 500 times. Just after an hour of being here, I absolutely love it. I feel extremely loved, and I know this experience is going to be amazing, and I can't wait to share everything with you. I can just feel the power of the Spirit everywhere I go. I feel so blessed.

I hope to talk to you all soon! I'm not sure when my "P Day" is (free day), but I'll send an email as soon as I know with more information.

I love you all so much, and I'm grateful that Heavenly Father gave me such an extraordinary group of family and friends.

Much Love,

Sister Valerie Beckley

"Heaven is cheering you on today, tomorrow and forever."

Jeffrey R. Holland

The first night there, almost 3,000 missionaries at the Provo Missionary Training Center felt as if the whole word could hear our words, thoughts, chords, and prayers as we sang in the hope that we might help one soul come unto Christ. The power was within each of us.

We were there for two weeks—the next two weeks to bring hundreds more. While we gathered in the conference center together, all the missionaries listened to talks from several members of the Quorum of the Twelve Apostles as well as the Quorum of the Seventy. We felt the Holy Spirit move, and at the end of the conference, several thousand voices sang with full hearts "The Spirit of God," a hymn even I, a new convert, knew by heart because it was still my favorite hymn.

It moved me and made me feel nothing but good and wonderful things. I sang the words of truth with power in my voice and my heart. I sang with love. I felt in my heart that God had led me this far, and that I wouldn't be abandoned.

"The Spirit of God like a fire is burning!
The latter-day glory begins to come forth;
The visions and blessings of old are returning,
And angels are coming to visit the earth."

We all took a breath and thought of the wonderful mission the Lord had called us on in separate parts of the world. I looked around the room at the handful headed to Australia or other states in the US, others learning new languages and headed to Africa, South America, Africa, Europe, and Asia. I looked at my new companion for two weeks, Sister Greg. We both smiled as the entire missionary training center burst into the next stanza of the powerful hymn. I did not know her well yet, but we were both there to serve the Lord. That was enough to make me love her and love what we were on task to do together.

"The Lord is extending the Saints' understanding,
Restoring their judges and all as at first.
The knowledge and power of God are expanding;
The veil o'er the earth is beginning to burst."

I grinned and continued to breathe in fresh air and sing with more gusto than I ever had in choir at school.

"We'll sing and we'll shout with the armies of heaven,
Hosanna, hosanna to God and the Lamb!
Let glory to them in the highest be given,
Henceforth and forever, Amen and amen!"

I then sang louder than before, wanting to let Heavenly Father know how excited I was to be here, serving the Savior. Tears flowed messily as I belted out the next stanzas. We all sang the last couple of verses together in the most powerful unison I had ever heard:

"How blessed the day when the lamb and the lion
Shall lie down together without any ire,
And Ephraim be crowned with his blessing in Zion,
As Jesus descends with his chariot of fire!"

I had chills. I stood silently and listened as the rest of the packed missionary training center sang the final stanza, humble and strong.

"We'll sing and we'll shout with the armies of heaven,
Hosanna, hosanna to God and the Lamb!
Let glory to them in the highest be given,
Henceforth and forever, Amen and amen!"

I cried silently as I took in the beautiful music of those going forth to serve, including myself—a part of it all. I thought of my entire journey so far.

We sat down after the powerful song was finished, and we prayed along with the prayer leader. *What a wonderful night this has been. What a wonderful truth I have known.* I wanted everyone to know it—to know the truth.

Over 150 people received each weekly email I was able to send. Church family, West Virginia family, and the Parker family all got my updates, along with pictures, study notes, and testimony. I hoped and prayed that my family could feel the Spirit through my emails, smile, and stories. I felt new, improved, and ready to serve.

Subject: First "P Day" Email

Hi everyone! This is my third day at the MTC, and I seriously love it. Let me tell you a little bit about my experiences thus far. (Also, I'll be able to email every Friday at the MTC for the next two weeks. And then I'll be in Texas and that day will change.)

Anyway, the Spirit at this place is unbelievable. Seriously! Everyone is so passionate about missionary work and their purpose. I love being around so many inspiring people my age. My companion is named Sister Greg. She is from Provo, Utah, and I love her already. She is so cool! She is a soccer player, and before the mission she did one year at BYU

Hawaii. She has a lot of courage to leave Hawaii and go on a mission. She helps me in so many ways. She helps me to drink more water and eat a little healthier, which I'm grateful for. Eating well helps with the early-morning and late-night schedule we are asked to follow.

My district is a group of elders and sisters (ten of us), and we go to class together all day. They are like my siblings, and it is so fun! They have fantastic personalities. There's Elder Chase and Elder Smith, who are companions; Elder Jenkins and Elder Tucker, who are companions; and then there's Elder Brooks and Elder Richards. They are awesome. And then Sister Greg and I are companions, and the last set is Sister Warren and Sister Paige. We do everything together. We pray together, eat together, go to the temple together, and we go to class and devotionals together too. It is wonderful to always have people there to strengthen and encourage you.

The first day at the MTC, we had to teach an actual investigator. This was so scary. About one hundred missionaries listened to the story of this woman who was interested in the Church. We all tried our best to teach her and share our knowledge. I stayed in my seat, being scared, but toward the end of the lesson I realized I could say something about my testimony and about my conversion to the LDS church that would really open her eyes and help her understand what everyone else was trying to tell her. I shared a piece of my story, and she was in tears. I realized how important it is for me to be here. The struggles I have been through and the trials God has given me are for these people that I'll teach. It helps me to relate to them and help them. I love my testimony, and I love that God has blessed me with one!

Yesterday was a long day full of classes and getting the hang of things. I was asked to share my testimony this Sunday on Fast Sunday where we all fast for about ten hours or so and then go to church. Instead of talks given, we share what we love about the Church and the gospel and what we believe to be true. It is fun but also scary, in front of all those people.

Today is my P Day. Woohoo! Today we clean our rooms, exercise, email home, do laundry, and walk around. We also, as a district, went to the Provo temple this morning. It was beautiful.

I love being a missionary. I love wearing a name tag that places responsibility upon me to act as a disciple of Christ. I love the things they teach us here. I can't wait to invite others to come unto Christ by helping them receive the restored gospel through faith in Jesus Christ and His Atonement, repentance, baptism, receiving the gift of the Holy Ghost, and enduring to the end. I can't wait to share that with the people of Fort Worth, Texas!

I'm blessed to have this communication with all of you, and I miss you so much. I have been told many times by many people that this mission I'm serving will bless myself and those that I teach, BUT I know that the time that I'm giving to the Lord and His children will also bless all of you! Do everything you can to become closer to Him! It is the most desirable of all things, and I know that He wants the best for all of us. Thank you all for loving me and supporting me. It is all I can ask for.

I love you all more than life. Talk to you soon!

Until Next P Day,

Sister Valerie Beckley

"Heaven is cheering you on today, tomorrow and forever."

Jeffrey R. Holland

Chapter Ten

BLINDED BY THE LIGHT

"There is no grief like the grief that does not speak."
Henry Wadsworth Longfellow

AUTUMN

THAT FIRST P DAY, I got several emails from my family, the Parker family, and the brothers and sisters in the ward from Arizona. I scrolled to the bottom of the list to reply to those who had reached out first in hopes that I would be able to hear back from everyone. While at the MTC, all missionaries were on emailing schedules so that everyone could use the computers and communicate with friends and family. We had an hour in the morning and an hour before P Day ended at dinnertime to do so. On that day, the first hour flew by; the last hour felt like an eternity of confusion and pain.

I scrolled through emails when Sister Greg and I went back to the computer lounge before dinner for our last hour. When I got to the top, I saw I had received an email from Sarah with a subject line in which she prompted me to open the email with caution. My stomach turned.

The message wasn't long, but it made me want to throw up and cry all at the same time. My eyes blurred, and I placed my hands in my palms as sobs poured while Sister Greg read along.

Subject: Val, open with caution . . .

Hey Val, it's Sarah. I'm sending this from class because I just found out some news that you may want to brace yourself for. They announced on the intercom this morning that Thomas lost his life in a car accident yesterday. I know you and Jayce both were close with him, and since you don't talk with many people back here anymore, I thought I would let you know. I am sorry, Val. I miss you and I am grateful for you. Wish you could come home.

Sarah

Subject: RE: Val, open with caution . . .

Sarah, this did hit hard. Thank you for letting me know. I love you and miss you.

Val

I immediately started crying. I thought about emailing Jayce, but we hadn't talked in so long, and what was I going to say? Sarah and Mia had been emailing me a bit about what was going on back at Mountain Valley High. Even though I hadn't been in direct contact with Jayce, my family still loved him and had kept me up to date. He and Thomas had been in their first year at Shepherd University, living it up and enjoying their new freedom. Thomas had really started coming into his own as an assistant football coach at Mountain Valley—his players loved him. And now this had happened.

My heart continued to break for what I knew Jayce must be feeling.

I didn't respond to any more emails that day. I cried and prayed with Sister Greg.

"I am so sorry, Sister Beckley. I hope you know I'm here for you. What do you think about getting a priesthood blessing?"

"That may help."

My thoughts ran wild regarding everything but being a missionary. *Jayce is going be a wreck.* I wished I could talk with him and cry with him. Thomas was like his brother. My chest felt heavy as Sister Greg and I searched for some of the senior couple missionaries along with Elder Brooks and Elder Richards from our district to perform the blessing.

We all gathered for a blessing of peace and comfort. I sat, and the elders placed their right hands on my head and their lefts on the shoulders of the brothers next to them. Elder James, a high priest and senior couple missionary, was chosen to give the blessing.

"Sister Valerie Beckley, this blessing is being given under the authority of the Melchizedek Priesthood. You are loved, cherished, and supported by your Father in Heaven to serve a mission in Texas. You will bless, teach, and serve many as you act selflessly in the service of our Lord and Savior, Jesus Christ. He wishes that you might not waver in your steadfast faith, and that you would press forward despite the news you have received today. As you have studied, you know that Thomas will have the opportunity to find the true gospel, even though he is gone. The Savior and Heavenly Father have provided a way for all to know the truth if they so choose. May you have peace and joy knowing that Thomas will get that chance to hear the perfect gospel and come unto our Savior. I place this blessing upon you, that you may have comfort, peace, and love in your heart, in the name of Jesus Christ."

I thanked the elders for performing the blessing. I did feel peace and comfort. Not joy, though. I didn't feel joy. I wondered why I felt that way but quickly put it out of my head. Elder James was right; I did need to remain focused on my mission, and Thomas would still get a chance to be saved. There was nothing I could do at this point besides pray—pray for Thomas, Jayce, and their families. So I did. I hoped they could feel my prayers.

I only briefly mentioned the situation in my emails home. I had no contact with Jayce or Thomas's family, so I fasted, that they might feel the same peace and comfort I felt.

Subject: P Day Email: 2 more weeks until Texas!

Hi everyone! This week has been crazy to say the least. Sunday, Fast Sunday. We fast two meals to focus on something that we really want to pray for. I fasted for a lot of different things, but my main fast was for Thomas's loved ones back in West Virginia. I found out last Monday that he passed, and it broke my heart. I received a blessing from the elders and continue to pray and fast for Thomas's loved ones: his friend who was like a brother, his family, and those who he was coaching on the football team. I also fasted for my family and my friends. I know everyone will hear about the gospel when they are ready, including Thomas. It is in God's plan, and it is such a perfect plan.

When I woke up Sunday morning before I began to fast, I was sick. I had a terrible cough and a sore throat and some other symptoms like chills. Unfortunately, the doctor was not in on Sunday or Monday, so I had to wait two days. The next few days were hard, but I got through them. I got Sister Greg sick too. That is unavoidable when you are in the same room! We both fasted anyway and prayed that the Lord would give us strength during that trial so we could fast accordingly.

On Tuesday we went to the doctor, and it turns out we just had a bad head cold. We took our medicine, went to bed for about forty-five mins, and we couldn't stand not doing anything! We put our skirts back on and headed back to our schedule. My cold is starting to go away, and I'm grateful for that.

Tuesday night I sang with my whole district in the choir when Brother Christofferson (one of the Twelve Apostles) came to give us a devotional as well. It was amazing. He has such a powerful love for God, and it really showed as we listened to him. Later, I'll have to send some notes I took to share the message he brought!

This week my companion and I also got two investigators who are interested in joining the Church! They come onto the campus, and we teach them. It is awesome to get an idea of what it will be like in Texas with teaching people. We have one guy and one girl, and I have really loved connecting with them, relating with them, and learning how to teach them about the gospel that brings me so much happiness.

I hope to hear from all of you! I have a lot of laundry to do today, but I'll make sure to respond to everyone. I love you all so much, and I'm so grateful for you in my life.

Love always,

Sister Valerie Beckley

"Heaven is cheering you on today, tomorrow and forever."

Jeffrey R. Holland

Subject: Taking off to Texas, Y'all!

Hi everyone! About an hour after I sent my last P Day email, I received my travel plans for Texas. I leave in three days. My flight takes off at 8:30 a.m., and I should land in Texas at noon. The MTC has been amazing, but I'm so eager to get to work!

Sunday was awesome! Sister Greg and I were chosen to be the sister training leaders of our zone. We oversee about twenty sisters and make sure they are always doing okay and answer any questions they have, check on them before bed, stay with them if they are sick, etc. So that is super great, and I have gotten to know the girls so well because of that responsibility. Also, on Sunday, we had another apostle come to speak to us at our Sunday devotional. M. Russell Ballard came and shared some great thoughts that I wanted to share with you:

*Forget yourself and love God and people. If you do, you'll be a powerful tool for good.

*Be dedicated from the tips of your toes to the top of your head.

*We are tools in the Lord's hands, and we carry His light.

*You receive no witness until after the trial of your faith. (Ether 12:6)

*The worth of souls is great in the sight of God. (Doctrine and Covenants 18:10)

He is wise, and I loved hearing from him!!

This week we got new investigators, Barbra and Olivia. They have incredibly sweet spirits! I have had to pray hard and study a lot to teach them, but it has been a valuable experience.

We got two new districts on Wednesday, and we gave them a tour of the MTC, which was fun. Some of the ones we got to meet are headed to Canada, California, and Arizona. They are so passionate about missionary work!

This week on Tuesday, the devotional was amazing! We sang in the choir again, and it brought the Spirit strongly. ANOTHER apostle came (we are lucky to have heard from three of them during our training), and here are some things I liked from Quentin L. Cook, and his wife Mary:

*Glady, I'll walk in the light.

*He isn't protecting us from pain; He is perfecting us through it.

*The Savior's Atonement covers all the unfairness of life.

*Doctrine and Covenants 31:3: Lift up your heart and rejoice, for the hour of your mission is come; and your tongue shall be loosed, and you shall declare glad tidings of joy unto this generation.

This week, Sister Greg got enough Dr. Pepper and double chocolate salted cookies in the mail to share, and it was amazing.

Thursday was the longest day of the week for sure. It was the "In-Field Orientation Day." We practiced things that we will be doing on our missions: meetings, door approaches, street contacting, etc. It was a long day, but it was full of information, and it helped us all to be less nervous and made us excited to go into the field.

Words can't accurately express how much I love this gospel. It has changed my life and made me so joyous during challenging times. I can't wait to instruct people and dedicate this next eighteen-month period to serving the Lord's children. If any of you have any questions about anything in my emails, feel free to ask! I miss you all so much, and I'm grateful for you in my life. Your emails and letters mean the world to me, and I couldn't ask for a better support system.

Much love,
Sister Valerie Beckley
"Heaven is cheering you on today, tomorrow and forever."
Jeffrey R. Holland

Before leaving the next day on our separate missions around the world, the hundreds of prepared yet unprepared new missionaries gathered for one last conference. We received encouragement, prayer, and hymns to move us on our way in faith. The last hymn we all sang together was a recent compilation of both "Sisters in Zion" and "We'll Bring the World His Truth." The sisters began. We all sang together, all sopranos, mezzos, and altos in perfect blend. I knew all the words and was proud to sing along. It felt wonderful, surreal but so truly real. We were missionaries headed out into the world to spread the truth of the gospel as sisters and brothers. The women sang about working together, strengthening the weak, and the strong love held for Heavenly Father.

This song was two songs mixed; therefore, the chords changed slightly, preparing for the next section and tone of the song. There was a piano break before the elders began to echo our faithful hymn together as the piano and all other instruments changed rhythm.

Never once did I think of those who might oppose what I believed now. It was simply truth. It was beautiful and wonderful, and my testimony continued with the music that I wholeheartedly listened to. The elders began to sing about following the commandment to deliver the truth of the gospel to the world.

I listened to them sing. I cried silently. I hadn't been taught in my youth, but I knew now the truth they sang of—we sang of. I thought of my life in retrospect and couldn't be more grateful for where I was in this moment. The missionaries came to me, and now I was being sent to others.

I pondered that thought as we moved back into the women's part. I smiled, and the melodies merged together in a glorious ring of music that would honor God, without a doubt.

All several thousand voices, male and female, in the MTC rang together to tell the world that we would soon be bringing the world the truth.

The piano echoed as the voices softened, and we all sat for a prayer that would move us forward into our missions for the Lord. We were setting out, and we were ready. I had learned the truth. I knew it was true, and I had felt it. I wanted everyone to feel the love that I felt and the truth that came with it.

Subject: First P Day in Texas

Hey, y'all! So, Texas is great! It is humid here, but it feels amazing. I'm in a town called Decatur, and my new companion, Sister Hills, and I are also covering the surrounding towns. Decatur is a super-cute town, and it has an old water tower, old diners, and an old mansion on the hill. It is a poverty-stricken area with a few wealthy families. Nonetheless, this town makes me feel at home, and I can tell you that Southern hospitality is a real thing and I have been blessed by it since I have been here.

Many of you will laugh at the thought of this, but I'm the designated driver between me and my companion, and I'm driving a white Nissan Frontier, which is a truck. The roads are rough in this area, and we have enough miles to cover, so I don't use my bike now, but I'm sure my time will come. Today we will be going to the store in Denton, a thirty-mile drive, and playing sports at the church building while we draft emails and such. It should be a nice relaxing day! We do this once a week, and the rest of the week we share messages of hope and the gospel.

My flight to Texas was great. I sat by two elders who were going there as well, and we had a friendly conversation. We got there, went to orientation for the day, and then we went to the mission home for dinner. We had brisket, potatoes, and Texas sheet cake. I have accepted the fact that I may gain a few pounds here. We then went to a member home, even though it was more like a mansion. It was a beautiful home, and before we went to bed, we had fresh cookies and made ice cream sandwiches with Blue Bell ice cream (my new obsession), and we all slept so well that night.

The next morning, the elders came to get us, and we drove to the church where I left Sister Greg and got my trainer (Sister Hills) and my new area. It was a bittersweet moment. That day we visited some recent converts and investigators, and we talked with them about the happiness the gospel can bring. That night we ate at the Butcher's home. We had ribs, double-baked potato casserole, and pumpkin cake.

The next day we had a lot of training and assignments that needed to be done, and we stayed inside most of the day. Sister Hills and I took breaks throughout the day, ate, and looked at pictures of our family and friends that we had both brought. That night, when we were heading back to our apartment, we needed gas and saw a gas station, but we didn't want to go to that one for some reason. Instead, we drove down the road to an Exxon, and there we met a family of seven and asked to meet with their family and talk to them about Jesus Christ. They said yes! I was so excited. I know God has perfect timing, and He knows who to bring into our lives when we or they need it most.

The next morning at 6:30 a.m., instead of doing our workouts, Sister Hills and I took a walk around the area and sat on a hill by the apartment and saw the sun rise! It was beautiful and a terrific way to spend the morning. That day we taught the family we met at the gas station. They want to know more about the gospel, and the kids get so excited when we come over. And the mom said, "Every time I'm going through a demanding time, y'all seem to pop up. Must be a sign from God, I guess." We are continuing to teach them, and I pray that they will be baptized together.

That night we ate at the Patricks' home, and since I'm a "greenie" (a new missionary), they made an all-green dinner—green pasta, green ice cream and green salad. It made me laugh.

Sunday, I shared my testimony in church, and we went to the

Davidsons' house for dinner. We then traveled to Denton for a fireside called "Why I Believe." There were many beautiful musical numbers, and then, to my surprise, they called me up on the stand to share my conversion story. No matter how far I go, and how many times I tell that story, I still cry every time, and the Spirit comforts me.

Being a missionary and sharing my testimony is the most important thing I can be doing right now. I miss my family, but I have seen lives change just in being here for five days, and I know with all my heart that this gospel can enrich anyone's life and make them happier and closer to God. I love my Savior, and I love that He knows us all by name. I'm grateful for Joseph Smith and that he was a tool in the Lord's hand in restoring the gospel. I know this church is true and is a blessing in my life, as it is in so many others'.

I miss y'all so much! I have all afternoon to email, so I'll try to get back to all of you. Monday is my P Day now, so that is the day I can email from ten to six, my time. However, send emails during the week because I can still read them, but Monday is my day to respond. Thank y'all so much for all the love and support you share with me. I'm grateful for you in my life.

P.S. Sorry this is long; I just had a lot to share. Missing everyone.
Much love,
Sister Valerie Beckley
"Heaven is cheering you on today, tomorrow and forever."
Jeffrey R. Holland

Several emails followed the first P Day email thread home to family, friends, and Arizona church members. Each week held more stories of baptisms, hardships, blessings, and the hope that everyone would feel the truth of the gospel through my emails—especially my family in West Virginia. Each week also held an immense amount of doors slammed, curse words yelled, and laughter at us riding our bikes when we did that, knocking on doors, and trying to share our message.

I especially hoped my family read my emails and thought about them. Even though we did not leave on the greatest terms, they now accepted what I had chosen to do. I just wanted them to understand why the Church was so great and how it had saved my life. I prayed every single night that they would feel the Spirit through my emails, since I could only talk to them on the phone or on FaceTime on Mother's Day and Christmas.

Months passed, and Christmas was approaching. My companion and I had taught the gospel and had several people agree to be baptized members in Decatur and the surrounding area. For several months, we had helped in communities and served the people who lived there. I had a feeling I would be transferred soon to experience a new area, and I knew I would miss Decatur and its memories, dear friendships, and the beautiful countryside. Its small-town feel reminded me of home.

I was looking forward to seeing everyone's faces via our FaceTime call on Christmas.

WINTER

Subject: Christmas Spirit

Hello everyone! This week, Sister Hills and I were challenged by our district leader to make the Sabbath day more special by doing something differently. So Sister Hills and I decided to make a big breakfast together. It is nothing spectacular, but it set the tone for a great Sunday. We made fresh muffins, eggs, hash browns, and sausage! We went to our meetings and then to church.

None of our investigators showed up for church, and none of them answered our texts. But that is okay; we'll still text them throughout the week and make brownies and cookies for them. I am sure they think we are annoying, but it's better than not caring, right? The talks in church were great. Some of the topics included the healing power of the Savior, Jesus Christ, and why God allows trials to happen to us and why they are for our benefit. In class we learned about doing the temple work for our ancestors who have passed away and haven't gotten the chance to learn about the gospel. It was a very enriching Sunday.

Think of something you can do to set Sunday apart from all the rest as a day to focus on the Atonement of Jesus Christ and what He has done for us. I promise that if you do this, you will see a difference in your relationship with the Savior and a new perspective on the Sabbath day the Lord has asked us to keep holy. I know it will bless your life immensely.

Sister Hills and I have also decided to wake up and continue exercising and getting ready for the day as usual, and then go to the church to study for about three hours. We could always study at our apartment; however, we love the Spirit of the Church, and there are so many great resources in the library, and we both love actual books rather than our tablet. We feel like that will strengthen us and our testimonies and will start doing that tomorrow. We are excited to be more engaged in the scriptures and studying! As always, people reject the message through door slams, or hurtful comments, but we still press on in faith and know that those ready to hear the gospel will hear us out.

I'm missing everyone and can't wait to talk to some of y'all on Christmas in only five days! This week, while Sister Hills and I went looking for investigators, we ran into an old Dr. Pepper advertisement painted on the side of a building in Decatur, so that was a neat find.

We have also been teaching an upcoming eight-year-old who wants to be baptized. We love teaching her because it helps us to remember to teach the gospel simply, because it is truly so simple!! I love the simplicity of the gospel.

I hope to hear from all of you today! I miss y'all so much!
Much love,
Sister Valerie Beckley
"Heaven is cheering you on today, tomorrow and forever."
Jeffrey R. Holland

Subject: Hello from West Virginia

Hey, Val, it is Dad. I hope you're having a fun week. There's a Christmas package on the way for you and your companion. I hope you receive it soon. It is a different world without you, and we all miss you. I hope you know how loved you are and how much I wish things could go back to the way they were. I hope you are safe, healthy, and feeling love from us, even if we are far. Merry Christmas!

Love you always,

Dad

Subject: RE: Hello from West Virginia

Dad! I miss you also and think of you all the time. Please send any photos! I miss everyone and love seeing all that is happening. That is so sweet you sent a package. Tell Renee I said thank you as well. Sending all my love and Christmas cheer!

Love always,

Val

Subject: VAL!!

Hi Val! Mia here. I know we haven't talked in quite a while, but Dad and I were eating breakfast this morning and we were talking about how weird it is without you and being able to talk with you more often. I don't understand it all, but you seem happy. I just wanted to let you know I love and miss you. Merry Christmas!

Mia

Subject: RE: Val!!

Hey, Mia! I sure do miss you too. I hope school is going well for you in West Virginia. How was homecoming this year? How are the dogs? Have you had the first snow yet? Send pictures of everything! It makes me feel like I'm there. Missing you but feeling happy to do the Lord's work this Christmas. I love you so much!

Love always,

Val

Subject: Missing You

Hi Val, it is Nan and Gramps. We just wanted to say we are thinking of you and are proud of all you have done. We don't understand why this mission takes you away from your family . . . anything that takes you away from your family can't be good, right? We are willing to support you. We just miss you, dear. I hope you know how loved you are. Merry Christmas, sweetie.

Love forever,

Nan and Gramps

Subject: My Sweet Daughter

Hey there, it's Mom. Here are some photos from the week. I went on a trip with Paul the other day. We had our first snow, and we bundled up to go skiing. It was a blast. You would have had a fun time. I just wanted to say that we miss and love you, Val. We think of you every day. I'm sending photos of the snow, of our newest edition, Ranger the golden retriever, and of what our home looks like decorated for Christmas. It isn't the same without you, but I wanted to send it your way. I know when you send me photos, it makes me feel like I'm with you, so I hope these do the same. I love you, sweet girl. Merry, merry Christmas.

Love always,

Mom

Subject: RE: My Sweet Daughter

Mom, thank you for these. They truly made my week. I miss you terribly. Please tell Paul the same, and that I love you both. I know this gospel is true, but it is hard being away from family. You're right, I would have loved to go skiing. I'll for sure go when I visit home after my mission. I love you, Mom. Merry Christmas. Thanks for keeping me in your thoughts and prayers.

Love,

Val

Subject: Weekly Update

Hello all! Something I realized Wednesday: life isn't going to be perfectly planned out. That is something I have always struggled with. I'm the girl who always carries an old-fashioned planner, lists, and schedules everything. This is important, but I took it too seriously. You must leave room for the Lord's will in there too. So I've learned that real life is doing your best to plan but being all right and adaptable when it falls through or doesn't work out. Having that knowledge has helped me so much. I'm a whole lot calmer, and I feel more at peace.

Regarding the rest of the week, Thursday, we had a long weekly planning session in the apartment. Friday, we went to a place called Harvest House for service in the morning. It was fun. The organization sends out packages of food to families in need.

I love being on a mission. It is hard, without a doubt, but you learn so much and adapt to many different situations. What a blessing to learn all these things in such a short amount of time!

Much love,

Sister Valerie Beckley

"Heaven is cheering you on today, tomorrow and forever."

Jeffrey R. Holland

Despite my mostly cheerful emails, after I FaceTimed my family on Christmas, nothing was the same. I missed them so much that it started to break my heart.

I said goodbye to everyone in the Decatur ward when transfers came after Christmas. I would miss them, and my companion, Sister Hills. They profoundly changed the first part of my mission and made me a better missionary. I learned so much from their examples and kindness.

I had three companions after Sister Hills. The first one was sweet: Sister Cook challenged me and made me laugh more than anyone

I had ever met. She was from Alabama and brought an interesting view to the mission. Sister Justin was next. She was judgmental and tough to have a good relationship with. She grew up in Orem, Utah. She was kind to me much of the time, but we did not click.

She once told me, "That is such an immodest blouse" after seeing me in a photo I brought with me where I was wearing a tank top. Needless to say, I struggled with her. At one point, we were studying during our morning study time, taking a deep dive into some of the most prominent questions brough up by investigators in the Church. We did this to show we wanted to find the answers to their questions. These investigators were interested in polygamy and the questions that surrounded that part of the Church's history. We studied it, and we talked about it.

"If the prophet received revelation from Heavenly Father that men in the Church should take multiple wives again, would you question it? Or would you have faith?" Sister Justin asked.

My stomach turned at her disturbing question. I considered the commandments of following the prophet and his guidance but also the teachings of praying and asking God for answers for ourselves. While my mind was at war with this, I responded to Sister Justin.

"Well, no offense, Sister, but I would at least question it. That would be hard for me. And if I'm being honest, I don't agree with it," I responded.

Sister Justin was appalled, to say the least. She quickly said she would have faith and not question the prophet of God. She made me feel like a lesser missionary in the service of the Lord because she posed a question that I did not agree with.

"It may just be something you should pray about. I know Heavenly Father will give you peace and knowledge," Sister Justin said in an arrogant tone.

I faked a smile. Sister Justin was not saying she wanted plural marriage by any means; she was simply expressing that if the prophet came out with a declaration that it was to happen again, she would blindly follow without question. From that moment, I tried my best not to question things, but I couldn't help it. Was I blindly following?

Sister Justin and I were only together for one transfer, and then I got moved to be with Sister Ailine. I thanked Heavenly Father for that.

When I met Sister Ailine, I knew we would be good friends. She and her family lived in California, but they were all from Tonga. Her last name meant "bright, shining one" in Tongan. She was crucial in helping me as I grew uneasy about the things the Church had taken stances on that I did not agree with. I had the hardest time focusing because I missed everyone at home and being obedient was a hardship at times as well. Sister Justin's negativity and judgment had caused me to question so much, which did not help in my struggle. Mission life became more challenging and confusing. Sister Ailine struggled with the same things, and we helped and supported each other.

SPRING

Subject: First Day of Spring

Hey, y'all! Happy spring! This week was fun in my area with Sister Ailine. I have been here for a couple of months now, but it still feels new. We are covering two wards and two areas, so we are always busy.

One of the highlights of my week was serving the youth and their leaders at the wards we cover. The youth just returned from "trek," which is a three-day journey in the outdoors with handcarts, walking all day, eating humble food, all while dressed like pioneers. This experience is to remember and honor the pioneers that traveled west to establish the Church in the late 1800s. How cool is that?!

When they all got back, they were surprised by pizza and soda pop that the leaders had provided. We helped pick up all the pizzas and serve everything. It was a fun day. Some of the teenagers that had went on the trek shared their testimonies when they returned. That was powerful, and Sister Ailine and I also shared our testimony of the truthfulness of the gospel and the faith of the early pioneers.

Story of the week: We were out finding people who were interested. This is when we knock on doors and introduce ourselves. Often people listen and ask questions, but more often we get verbally pushed away and laughed at. At the end of the night, Sister Ailine and I went to a home with a minivan in the driveway and the lights on inside. A man answered the door and knew exactly who we were. He was not rude exactly. He had a lot say. He mentioned a lot of things that he obviously hadn't investigated. He told us in the kindest way possible that we were stupid for joining the Church and we hadn't studied or felt a true impression from the Holy Ghost.

I responded respectfully and as kindly as I could. "Joel, have you ever given yourself time to read the Book of Mormon?" He responded, "Not really. Mostly I've done a lot of research on other websites." We knew that he felt so negatively against the Church because he didn't go to the source. He hadn't read the book for himself. Personally, ever since reading the Book of Mormon, I have an even stronger testimony of the greatness of the Bible and the truthfulness of the Church! How could that not be from God?

To sum things up, I promised him that if he reads and truly prays with a sincere heart about the Book of Mormon, he will know if it is true or not! If he doesn't do that, I told him he would be going off his own understanding. The Bible says in Proverbs 3:5–6, "Trust in the Lord with all thine heart; and lean not unto thine own understanding. In all thy ways acknowledge him, and he shall direct thy paths." I explained that we must rely fully on our Father in Heaven, and He will show us the way. Joel was very set on his viewpoint, and we expressed that we all have our own opinions and gave him our phone number and told him that even if he was not interested in the Church, we would love to help him with anything we can if he ever needs it.

I'm grateful for this experience and the strength my testimony has gained. I know that nothing worthwhile will be easy.

We are on this earth, going through the trials we go through, doing what we must do so that the Savior can shape us! He wants us to learn from those trials and from our pains and lean unto Him and the Father for support and comfort. He loves all of us so much more than we can understand. Knowing that they love us and want us to learn and be shaped makes all the difference. It doesn't make trials go away, but it makes them bearable, and not only that, but with the Savior on our side and with the armies of heaven cheering us on, we have hope and happiness during our tough times.

I love the peace and knowledge that comes with learning more about the gospel. I'm beyond grateful to be serving a mission and learning all these truths every day, repeatedly, and teaching them. No greater joy comes than from serving Heavenly Father and His children! It is a blessing that is far too difficult for me to put into words. I'm overwhelmed with gratitude and thought I would share the things I have learned recently with y'all.

I miss all of you more than you know. I hope everyone is healthy and well. I look forward to emailing everyone today.

Much love,

Sister Valerie Beckley

"Heaven is cheering you on today, tomorrow and forever."

Jeffrey R. Holland

After sending that P Day email, I felt like I had lied to myself. I had read the Book of Mormon again recently and still felt it was true, but there were so many other thoughts going through my brain.

Subject: Another P Day Email

Sunday was of course the Sabbath day, and Mother's Day! We had church all day, which really brings the Spirit strongly. After church we got to call our families, which brought me so much joy.

It is crazy to think I only have one more FaceTime call home on Christmas, and then I'm mainly done with my mission. I have loved serving and look forward to continuing to do so here in Texas.

This will be a short email this week. I'll reach out individually to those who have sent emails. Thanks to everyone for the constant love, support, and encouragement. I'm incredibly grateful and blessed.

Much love,

Sister Valerie Beckley

"Heaven is cheering you on today, tomorrow and forever."

Jeffrey R. Holland

That was the shortest email I had sent so far, and I had a challenging time digesting what I had studied this week during morning study. I had been reading gospel topic essays and Joseph Smith history. Some things just did not line up. I also could not help but think of the conversation with Sister Justin from months ago. Ever since that conversation, I had been different. I was not blindly following anymore. I needed to figure things out for myself and find the truth.

Up until that point, I had been obedient with emailing strictly on Mondays during the designated time. Since Mother's Day, Sister Ailine and I both struggled with emailing our families during the week. We felt extremely guilty, but we missed them so much. Sister Ailine had a longer time left on her mission than I did, but realizing I had nine months left at this point made me miss everyone desperately. I was missing so much at home. Sarah was graduating high school, and Mia really missed me too, according to her emails to me. My heart had softened toward my family since going on my mission. I missed Arizona and the Parkers also, but my family was who I found myself emailing the most during the week.

The following Sunday was Fast Sunday. We fasted, prayed, and asked for guidance during these times of focus and dedication. Sister

Ailine and I knew each other's struggles. She knew I was missing home, and I knew she wanted to serve a successful mission but still be in contact with her family. We prayed that morning before church together and throughout the day for guidance and answers to our questions. That night, I asked Heavenly Father if I should go home or stay and serve. I did not receive a direct answer. If you were worthy of the Holy Ghost, His replies were always a bit easier to understand, but I did not feel worthy.

ALMOST SUMMER

Subject: Hello from West Virginia

Hey Val,

I'm sitting here tonight and wanted to start writing you a note for the week since your P Day is tomorrow. You have been on my mind all day today, and I just wanted to tell you that I love you. I loved being able to talk with you on Mother's Day, and I have thanked your mom for sharing that time.

I've been reminiscing about the early days when you, Mia, and I first moved to West Virginia from Georgia. The townhouse was our first home together after Nan and Gramps', and it was the first time in my life when I felt like I had done something on my own. Today, I would give anything to go back to 2005 and do it all again. I miss having you and Mia together, I miss doing your hair for school, I miss you getting irritated with Mia for trying to imitate you, and I miss driving around, watching you sing your favorite songs!

I feel like I have failed you over the years, and for that, I'm sorry. I know that you have made decisions based on the life you wanted to have, and you made decisions that you felt would put you in situations that would supply better opportunities, and I know that you are a strong, capable, and smart young woman, but I can't help thinking that if I had made different choices, things might be different for us today. I want you to know that I'm immensely proud of you, Val! I don't know how you became so thoughtful, so caring, and so generous, but I'm grateful that you did! You are a genuinely good person, and I love you so much!

My one regret is that I don't think I paid enough attention when you were younger. I know I was around and present for events like the shows for choir in school (which led to show choir), but I wish I had appreciated those times more than I did. Only today do I recognize how special those days were. I remember coming to your elementary school with Mia to have lunch with you and taking the two of you on the home tours around the county. For the life of me, I don't know how we ever started going to those, and I don't know why you enjoyed them so much, but I'm glad that you did. Between those tours and the Civil War sites, I feel like you should have become more of a geek!

I wish I could hug you right now. My heart hurts, and I can't wait to see you again. I think that Mia could use some time with you as well. We need to reconnect, and I can't wait until your mission is over so that we can do just that! I don't know what the future holds for any of us, or how things will be a year from now, but I do know that I'm grateful for the time that we have had together and for all the memories that we have made. I should not have allowed you to move in with your mom so easily back when you were in high school. I feel like once you moved out, our family became fractured, and we have never been the same since.

Anyway, enough self-pity. All I really need you to know is that I'm proud of you, I love you very much, and I can't wait to spend time with you and get to know you again as a young woman.

Sarah graduates on Thursday, so we have about four days until that. We are proud of her, but it breaks my heart you won't be there. Time goes by so fast! It seems like just yesterday that we were in Phoenix for your graduation. I miss you, Val. I hope you are well. Please let Renee and I know if you need anything at all.

Sending love,

Dad

I read that email from Dad that late Sunday in May. Usually, I could disconnect and just read, but I heard Dad in this one. I cried, and Sister Ailine hugged me and helped me figure out what I was feeling. Out of all the different kindhearted companions I'd had throughout my mission, Sister Ailine was the most down to earth. The two of us had a tough time being completely obedient, but we loved doing missionary work. She was real, and she was the one I trusted the most.

"I'm having a tough time being a missionary right now, Sister. I have a bad feeling."

"I know. Me too. What's making it so hard for you?" Sister Ailine asked.

"I just don't know if Joseph Smith was a prophet anymore. In our study time, I have been studying the Church's history a lot. I have found out things that don't really line up with how I feel in my heart. It just kills me to tell investigators, 'If you get baptized, you can't drink your coffee anymore.' They always ask why, and I always say that the revelation came from the prophet Joseph Smith, and that they just need to have faith in the commandment.

"I just don't know how I feel about it anymore. You know? And what about families? Why do we believe that if my family doesn't get baptized and go through the temple or choose it in the spirit world, I'll live without them in eternity? I don't want that. I don't want that for Thomas and his family, or Jayce and his family. I don't want that for anyone, and I don't think God would either. And I really don't want to be a blind follower, Sister. Also, and simply, I miss my home," Val finished.

"I get it. I have a tough time with the commandments and all that. I don't understand all of them, and that is all right. It's up to you to decide what is right for your life, Sister. You have changed my mission for the better. I hope you know that. You have helped me not miss my family as much. I still miss them, but you have helped with that. You've been a blessing. And I miss my family every day. I get it," Sister Ailine said.

"Sister Ailine, you have kept me on my mission this long. You are so kind, hilarious, and loving. Thank you for accepting my craziness and thank you for saying such kind things. You are one of my dearest friends. I just miss my family, and I have so many questions that I don't feel are being answered."

"Do you want to go home?"

"Yes. I have prayed about it a lot. I just don't know where to start."

"Let's call the mission president and his wife. I hate seeing you unhappy. We all deserve what we want in life. You want your family; go get them."

We called the mission president and his wife that night. It hurt my heart to tell them I was struggling with my testimony that was once so strong—to tell them I was too weak to not miss my family. They were soft and kind toward my request to go home. I was anxious, sad, and I needed to be with my family now that we were making amends.

Sister Ailine and I cried together again when we realized we would not be together more than a couple of days. I was so anxious about how to share the news with everyone. I started with Mom. I used the mission cell phone with permission from the mission president. When I told her I would be coming home and that I did not know many details besides that, she cried the happiest tears I had heard. She asked if I was going back to Arizona or West Virginia. That was when I told her I would be flying from Texas this week and I would be coming back home—to my West Virginia home. I also told the Parker family, all of whom had different reactions—no one disappointed, none making me feel judged for my decision; I was the recipient of nothing but love. How blessed I was.

Chapter Eleven

BACK HOME ON THE HILLS

*"Never say goodbye because goodbye means going away
and going away means forgetting."*
J. M. Barrie

SPRING

I WAITED UNTIL MONDAY to tell Dad.

Subject: RE: Hello from West Virginia

Hi Dad. I got your email. Big news, I'm coming home. I made the decision yesterday and was not sure if you were busy.

Love always,

Val

Subject: RE: Hello from West Virginia

Is everything okay? What brought this on?

Love you,

Dad

Subject: RE: Hello from West Virginia

Hey Dad, yes, everything is fine. I just feel like I should come home because I'm missing time with my family, and I have found out so much I don't agree with. It isn't like I don't trust that the Lord will take care of everyone. I just feel like I should be around. And I also feel that anything good won't truly take you away from your family . . . and a mission does that. I don't agree with limited communication with those who have supported me and helped me this far. I feel like the longer I stay on my mission, the more my testimony is weakening for some reason in terms of the Church. I just need time away. We all need that, I guess.

The mission president and his wife insisted on buying the ticket. I told them I would talk to you. I'm hoping to be there by Sarah's graduation.

Let me know what you think,

Val

PS Please don't tell anyone. I want it to be a surprise. I miss everyone so much.

Subject: RE: Hello from West Virginia

I feel like if you were fine, you would be staying, but I trust you. I'm so happy! I don't understand any of this, but I'm thrilled, Val, really. I miss you very much. I can't believe the Church is letting you leave your mission early! I won't tell anyone. If the mission president can get you home by her graduation on Thursday, that would be great, and if not, I can get the ticket. Just let me know.

Love always,

Dad

Subject: RE: Hello from West Virginia

Dad, the president said the Church will take care of the ticket and they would get me there Thursday. I'll send you flight details ASAP. I can't wait to hug you. I'm not sure what this will look like long term for my life, but I figure I'll have time on the plane to think about it.

See you soon,

Val

Subject: RE: Hello from West Virginia

Val, don't stress so much. You have more time to think than the time you have on the plane. Life is bigger than we know, and you always have time. I can't wait to see you, Val. My heart is happy.

My heart was happy, too.

Dad could not help but tell people I was coming home. I giggled when I realized he hadn't kept his promise because I was glad he was that excited to have me back in West Virginia. I sent an email to everyone at home to explain things a bit before jumping back into their lives.

Subject: Coming Home

Hey, y'all! As many of you know and have heard through the gossip, I'm coming home on Thursday. I can't wait to see and hug y'all. I can't believe I'm saying that so early! I have been here for nine months, and I have learned as a missionary that the only thing we can expect is change. Change is constant. I had no idea I would be coming home. I still don't know all the reasons I am doing so. I'm just acting on the prompting I have received and how I feel. I do know it won't be easy for me, but I'm so happy to regain normalcy and be with y'all. That is true happiness to me—being with family. And I can't wait.

My mission president and his wife have loved and supported me through this and helped me come home today. I'm so grateful for them and their Christlike love and service to me. I'm also grateful I have such a Christlike family. Y'all are my life, and I love you so much! Thank you for supporting me always, despite my crazy lifestyle of constant change, and despite not always knowing "why."

See you in a few short days!!! Mom, Dad, whoever picks me up at the airport, please bring tissues. I'll be a crying baby.

Ways you can help me upon my return:

Keep me busy. Missionary life is constantly going, and if I sit still too long, I'll become depressed, so even if you're just running errands, I'll want to go and help.

I'll have to report my mission to the ward leaders when I return home. This will be different since I won't be returning to Arizona right away. I plan to fly there in a couple of weeks to do the same. It is the duty of a missionary, and even though I didn't finish my eighteen-month mission, I do still have to report to my ward there as well. They have truly given me so much love, so many experiences, and so much encouragement along the way. It will break my heart to tell them my testimony is struggling.

Keep me positive. These decisions are weighing heavily on my heart, but I have received my personal answer, and I'm excited to return to West Virginia. Also, we could feed the missionaries dinner one night. Idk if there are elders or sisters in our area, but we will see. I'll cook! I'm a decent cook now. Texas taught me well. I sure will miss it.

Thanks for everything. I can't wait to see everyone in a couple of days.

Love always,

Val

Again, I was lying to myself. I knew I had a problem with my testimony of the truthfulness of the Church. I just did not want everyone knowing that because I was still trying to understand it.

All this time, I had thought the Church was true. It might have been, but there were so many questions and issues I couldn't resolve.

Why couldn't I be allowed to be with my family forever if they thought the Church was not true? Nan was right. Anything worthwhile would not take you from your family. I just needed time to figure it out for myself instead of preaching the gospel to others.

I met up with the mission president and his wife on that warm Texas morning at the end of May. Prayers were said, tears were shed, and hugs were given. Texas and the people there had become a part of my heart, one of the dearest parts. I left with a heavy spirit that morning but was still full of hope for what was to come. I also was sad to think that people I had served with would think harshly toward me for leaving early. It was embarrassing for many who did, but not for me. I was ready, and that was okay. I was anxious about reporting my mission in West Virginia and Arizona. But for now, I would have time to myself on the plane to ponder what life held for me next.

I boarded my flight to Regan International with my missionary tag still on my shirt. I would have it on until I reported my mission, which was scheduled to happen tonight after Sarah's graduation. I would be picked up by Mom, who I was almost positive had not slept since I told her I would be coming home.

I thought about a lot on the plane that morning. Returning early from a mission received differing responses. Little did I know, very few people would talk to me after that. The Parker family never stopped making me feel loved. I felt so blessed to know them. I thought about Jayce, and Thomas, and all my girlfriends that I had lost contact with since my mission began nine months ago. I thought about what had changed since I left. I needed to prepare myself for a whole different world; I was going to be a stranger in it for a while.

I was not set on leaving the Church, but Joseph Smith was not a prophet to me anymore after learning so much about him. *I know that no one is perfect, but I also know that someone called of God would not do some of the things that he did, as well as those who came after him in that role as prophet, seer, and revelator.* I thought about how my family had to be baptized into the Church for us to be sealed together for all time and eternity. I hated that. *Do I even believe in the Church if I think Joseph Smith was not a prophet? Is that even possible?* I knew it was not, but I tried to think otherwise, because for the last two years it was all I had known and embraced. I almost forgot all other beliefs and ways of thinking.

"Good afternoon, passengers. We are sending the flight attendants around to pick up any loose trash as we get ready to land in the nation's capital. Please put your seats and tray tables in the upright position and secure your seatbelts. It is about eighty-one degrees in Washington today as we prepare for landing, and the sun is shining. Thank you for flying with us today. We wish you the best and hope to see you again soon."

My heart started racing at the anticipation of seeing my mom. It had been about a year now since I graduated and hugged her that last time. I was thrilled. I grabbed my missionary shoulder bag as we landed, collected myself, and walked as fast as I could to baggage claim, where she would be waiting.

When I saw her blonde hair, giant white smile, and the sign she had made to welcome me home, I dropped everything I had in my arms and ran to her. That hug, I hoped, made her feel all good things—because that was how I felt toward her. I hoped in that hug filled with tears she felt my gratitude for her being my best friend. I couldn't wait to hug Dad, too. And Mia. And everyone.

We gathered my things as I talked her ear off. We went on our way, and she dropped me off at Dad's house for Sarah's graduation. When I knocked on the door and Dad answered, it was as if in that moment, everything that had happened was washed away. I was home, and my dad was crying again. This time he was crying tears of joy to have me home.

I couldn't remember if I had cried that much since leaving for Arizona two years before. Maybe when I heard about Thomas. So much had happened, and I had gotten hard when I thought I was becoming more loving and accepting. My hard walls broke down bit by bit as I greeted each family member. Sarah was already at graduation practice, so seeing me there would be a surprise for her. Mia screamed as I swung her around in a hug. She even shed a tear and said, "I'm really glad that you're home, Val."

I responded, "Me too, Mia. Me too" as I hugged her again. Mia did not cry often, so that meant a lot. Renee came downstairs in tears as well. She hugged me so hard and told me she was sorry for making things challenging before. I hugged her back and said I would like to start fresh.

It was overall a good homecoming. I was nervous to see Nan and Gramps, and I was also nervous to make an appearance at Mountain Valley's graduation. I was anxious about who I might run into.

Dad, Mia, and I hopped into the car to visit Nan and Gramps. Dad rolled down the windows, and we drove down backroads that I remembered like the back of my hand. Those roads felt comforting for once in my life, yet they also reminded me that coming home meant starting over again. It thrilled and terrified me at the same time.

I zoned out for most of the drive across town. Dad was playing *American Beauty*, one of the best albums of all time. It felt good to listen to the Grateful Dead without the fear of Heavenly Father being disappointed in what I was listening to anymore. It felt good to hear anything on the radio. We could not listen to anything besides church music on our mission. I thought of Sister Ailine and the times we would turn on the regular radio, feel bad, and then quickly play hymns. I missed her, but I knew she would be all right.

"What a long, strange trip it's been," the three of us sang as we cruised down the twisting roads, laughing at the irony of the lyrics.

The house I'd grown up in looked the same, though a bit brighter than before. It seemed to glow as we walked in. Knocking was not a thing that anyone besides the occasional new FedEx worker did at Nan and Gramps.

They asked a million questions as we hugged, and cried as well. I laughed and told them it would all work out, but for now I was home. I would be over soon to talk about everything, but we had to get to Sarah's graduation. They both gave me another giant hug as I promised I would be back to catch up. Gramps hugged me a little longer than normal, once again with tears in his eyes. Nan's eyes were bright with tears as well; this time, they were both happy crying. Everyone's hard walls were coming down, including mine.

We drove back toward Mountain Valley and picked up Renee, who had finished getting ready, as well as John, who had been playing video games and did not hear me come home earlier. He gave me a bear hug and we all drove to Sarah's graduation.

"Val, there are so many great songs that have come out since you've been gone. Are you staying the night tonight? Maybe we could catch you up on movies and music," Mia said.

"That is pretty true. There have also been a few video game releases. Wanna see those, too?" John asked. Mia and I giggled. He knew we had no interest in his gaming.

"I would love to see what the new games are," I responded seriously with a smile.

"Yes!" John exclaimed at my unexpected answer.

"But you have to let Sarah and I catch you up on music and movies also," Mia insisted.

"I think it all sounds great. I can do all of that once I get released as a missionary tonight after the graduation. I'll go to Mom's tomorrow morning when you go over for your weekend with her, Mia."

So that was settled. I was going to the missionary release with Mom and Dad, who wanted to be a part of it. I did not know what to expect. My testimony was struggling, but I could give a strong witness of what had happened for the nine months I was in the service of the Lord. I was grateful I had done it, and I would gladly say that. I was still nervous about their reactions.

Mountain Valley High School felt oddly familiar. I was not expecting to connect with the school I had once wanted so badly to escape, but as I saw my old English teachers, principal, and friends visiting town for the summer months ahead, I felt a little more at home. I shed a few tears when I saw a photo of Thomas and Jayce in the gym hallway: the photo of their first winning touchdown they both assisted, years ago—helmets in the air and smiles wide.

Dad, Renee, John, Mia, and I went to our seats in the bleachers to await the graduates lining up for their diplomas. I chatted with Mia as I looked around the gym. My eyes landed on Jayce and his family in the bleachers. He was already looking back at me. My heart beat quickly and nervously in that moment. I wondered why he was here. He looked distracted and less bright in the face. Mia had told me he was going to one of the local colleges down the road near the Potomac River. I wished I could talk to him, but it had been so long. I looked away and pretended not to notice.

The ceremony started, and Sarah graduated as a student athlete headed to college. We were overjoyed for her. I kept looking over at Jayce, and eventually, when Jade Ripple was called to graduate, Jayce's family began hooting and clapping for her. My heart sank. I knew in that moment that Jayce had moved on. I could not blame him. We had stopped writing each other a year and a half ago, and so much had happened after I left.

After the ceremony, Sarah and I hugged and cried. I had missed her sweet soul and was so proud of her. We had not talked much while I was gone on my mission, but I hoped she still felt loving toward me. I felt like she did. I felt like in that moment that I had made everything right.

And not only did I feel like I had made everything right, but I also felt like we had all grown. Mia told Sarah about our plans for catching me up on pop culture later. She had an after-party to go to, but she said she would be home soon. In the meantime, I went to my mission release at the local ward building.

Though I was unfamiliar with the ward in West Virginia and felt as if these people did not know me at all, I gave a stirring witness of all the wonderful people I had met and the experiences I'd had in Texas.

I wasn't sure what the future would hold, but I wasn't going to say I believed in the Church and all those other things that believers said. I just couldn't. I said that I had the time of my life, teaching, loving, and serving. I learned about people, cultures, and diverse ways of life. I said that I learned to love those who believed differently than myself, and that I learned to listen to my heart.

I said that I learned something invaluable —that I wasn't alone in the world, no matter the phase I was in. I said I knew that Heavenly Father loved me. I said that I felt purposeful and loving. I said that I was grateful that my mission had taught me things I did not understand before.

That was it. Nothing about the current prophet, nothing about Joseph Smith, nothing about the true gospel of Jesus Christ being restored, and nothing about anything else besides my truth.

I think the best thing that came of that meeting was the fact that afterward, I knew in my heart that the Church was not for me. It hurt because in a lot of ways, my life had changed for the better because of the Church. My mission changed me for the better.

I then went on my way with my family. I called Amelia, who was with Gram in Arizona. I needed to call them and tell them how I felt.

"Hello?" the double voice echoed on speakerphone.

"Amelia! Gram! How are you? I miss y'all."

"We are good, sweetie. We miss you too. The more important question, though, is how are you?" Gram asked.

They did not know the degree to which I was struggling with my testimony yet. They knew I had left and come home, but I had not expressed why.

"I'm good. Sarah's graduation was great. Everyone was excited to see me. I was grateful to be greeted by so many loving arms. Leaving Sister Ailine was tough. I really loved her. Being released as a missionary here was fine. I figured I would call before Mia and Sarah get me caught up on what movies, music, and shows have come out since I've been away."

"That will be so fun!" Amelia said.

"We really missed you, honey. Is everything okay? Will we get to see you soon?" Gram asked. I thought for a minute. I had not thought that far ahead, but it was fair to tell them that I was considering not being a member of the Church anymore and that the past few months had been a struggle for me.

"I missed y'all too. Everything is fine, but I discovered some things about the Church's history that I don't agree with, and I don't know if I'm willing to have faith in those things. I've had a challenging time with the doctrine lately."

They were silent, but I could tell they were not judging me; they were listening. I continued. "As much as I loved my mission and the past few years being in Arizona, I think I'm in need of some time away to focus on my family and finding who I am without the Church."

"We love you, honey. Thank you for telling us. I do think it'd be important for you to come to Arizona to report your mission to the ward leaders here, and of course we want to see you again before you start this new journey back in West Virginia. Do you think that could happen?" Gram asked.

"I wouldn't have it any other way."

"Great, just let us know what we can do to help, and you are welcome anytime. Keep us updated," Amelia commented. She had not talked much, which I understood. We had gotten so close because of the Church. Now I was leaving. I was sad as well, but simultaneously I felt joyful anticipation for what was next.

"I just want you both to know how much I love you."

Amelia and Gram both said that they loved me dearly, and that they looked forward to seeing me soon. We ended the call, and I considered a time to go there. I looked at flights, corresponded with Mom and Renee, and decided that I would leave at the beginning of the coming week to collect my things. Renee had said previously that she would fly out, rent a car, and we would drive back together. While she was working on that, I would report to my ward in Arizona, and say goodbye for now to everyone there who had supported me this whole time. I got anxious thinking about all the changes that I had weak explanations for and still struggled with.

Dad had ordered a new phone for me that was waiting at the house when I arrived earlier that day. I was grateful. I had never been addicted to technology, but I recognized that it had a way of connecting things that needed to be connected.

As I settled down to receive my movie and music education from Mia and Sarah, my phone lit up with a confirmation for my flight in a week. I put it into my calendar. I also got a notification from the extension office in my town, an email reminding all 4-H members that this was the last week to register for 4-H camp the following week—after I was scheduled to return from Arizona. I left the girls for a moment to talk to Dad and Renee about going. I had missed camp so much, and if I could go, I wanted to.

"I know that no one else would go with me, but I just got an email about the final week to turn in registration for 4-H camp. I would love to go. If it's okay with Mom, is that all right with you?" I asked them.

"That sounds fun! Absolutely," Renee said.

"How! How!" Dad exclaimed, something that 4-H members said when they were in favor of something. I smiled. The camp was separated into tribes based off the traditions of Native Americans in the West Virginia area. It was always a respectful, emotional, and exciting week to spend with good people who were in 4-H in the surrounding counties.

This was the last year I could attend camp because of my age, and I was going to be there with bells on. I did not technically have to ask my parents' permission, but I was in an awkward stage of needing some extra time to get on my feet, experience a couple of fun things over the summer, and then figure out a plan for what life would look like now. I think my parents did not care about this. They were simply at peace in knowing that I was home and was not going to be a member of the Church anymore. They were more than fine with my decision and were willing to support me as I figured out my next steps.

I had to accept that I would be doing things differently, at different times than other people. I was behind when compared to someone my age taking the traditional path to college and a career. I quickly realized that I needed to be capable of enjoying things such as my last year of 4-H camp, education, travel, and religion on my own, and in my own time.

That night, I learned many things about the world of recent music, film, and fashion. The past nine months of missionary service included long skirts, gospel music, and church movies—nothing more. It was enjoyable in a sense, but I was enjoying these new things now. We danced and sang to Jon Bellion's "All Time Low." It sounded nothing like the gospel music I had been listening to. I liked the gospel music, but this made my soul smile. Sarah then put on "Can't Stop the Feeling" by Justin Timberlake. The song made anyone and everyone want to dance. Thirty seconds into the song, Dad knocked on the door. We let him in, and his dancing shoes took the floor. He loved Justin Timberlake. We all giggled as he shuffled like we had never seen Dad shuffle before. My family and I danced together; no one was talking about religion or the complexities of life right now—we just danced. It was wonderful. We continued to listen to music, dance, and just be together.

We ended the night with popcorn and *The Choice*, a film adapted from the Nicolas Sparks novel while I was gone. My sisters knew I was a geek for romantic films. Even though I tended to run away from romance in my own life, I still enjoyed them and always ended up being the only one crying at the end. *Gosh, I hate these romance movies, but I love them at the same time.*

The movie made me think of Jayce. I quickly forced my mind to move on to other things. I had a lot to look forward to. I was going to Arizona to retrieve my things and see everyone, and I was going to attend my last year of 4-H camp.

We all fell asleep after the movie. It had been a long, rewarding day.

I rolled over when my body naturally woke me at 6:30 a.m., just as I had (most days) when I was serving my mission. Instead of fighting to wake up and study and exercise, I rolled back over for one more hour. Doing so made me feel powerful and relaxed. When I woke up an hour later, I made everyone breakfast, intent on sharing my newfound homestyle-cooking skills with my family, who loved eating out at restaurants. The aroma of biscuits and gravy woke them, and we ate breakfast together for the first time in a long time.

Mom came to get Mia and me. I brought her a plate of breakfast, and Mia and I said goodbye to everyone for the weekend. Mia would be back on Monday; she was still with Dad most of the time. I would see Renee in Arizona in only a few short days. I'd fly out on Monday, and Renee would be there by Wednesday to pack everything up and drive home with me.

The weekend with Mom included buying normal clothes and visiting Nan and Gramps. Mom, Mia, and I began our day at the mall. I still had my garments on under my clothes, which made me embarrassed and confused while trying on clothes. Temple garments were to be worn closest to the body. This meant that the bottoms acted as underwear, and any bra I wore had to go over the garment top. It had been this way for over a year now, and I was used to it. I had always dressed modestly, in my opinion. My promises in the temple to wear the garments did not change much besides the length of my shorts as well as sleeves on shirts. While shopping with Mom and Mia, though, I realized that I missed tank tops and sundresses. I'd had to make sure my garments were covered in whatever I wore.

I went in the dressing room alone as Mom and Mia looked through the store. The world seemed silent. Even the music in the mall faded away, the loudness of my mind overpowering it all. I stood in my temple garments, let my hair down from its tight bun, and looked at myself in the full-body mirror.

I had gained thirty pounds since moving to Arizona and serving a mission. The garments covered every section of my body that I felt was overgrown and unattractive, yet I felt so hidden and ashamed. I looked up and down at the stranger in the mirror and removed the garments.

I tried on all the outfits I had picked out and loved the way I felt in all of them. The next few moments made me feel like I was on top of the world. I bagged up my garments and put them in my purse, deciding to keep the new outfit on, shoulders showing and all.

"I will take these," I told the cashier. I bought the outfits that I wanted to buy, not the ones that met Church standards. "And here are the tags for what I put on after trying them on in the dressing room. I hope that's all right."

"Totally, that looks amazing on you," the cashier said.

I walked out of the store with a smile and showed Mom and Mia what I had bought. They said everything was cute and would suit me well.

"Wait a minute, you changed your outfit," Mia stated.

"Val, are you wearing your garments?" Mom asked. The outfit was not immodest—it was a thin-strapped jumper with stripes—but she knew that the outfit I was wearing would not be able to cover them.

"No, I'm not wearing them. They're in here," I said, holding up the bag from the store.

"Wait a second, aren't the garments your underwear?" Mia asked.

I looked at them and grinned.

"You're not wearing underwear? Valerie Beckley!" Mom jokingly scolded me.

We laughed loudly at the fact that after two years of being Mormon and one year of wearing garments, I was not wearing panties in the mall. We laughed a little too long, but it felt good.

"Why don't we go buy some real underwear?" Mom suggested.

"That is a great idea," I said. The white temple garments had replaced worldly pieces of fabric. Granted, the white holy cloth was one of the most comfortable things I had worn; however, they felt better in my purse. Elated and free, I no longer felt ashamed.

I think I knew in that moment that I was leaving the Church for good. I had broken my promises by taking off the garments. In my mind, I needed to keep every promise I had made in the temple or move on. I chose to move on.

After shopping, the three of us visited Nan and Gramps. They had glasses of sweet tea ready for Mia and me. They set down their wineglasses, gave us both big hugs, and sat us all down on the porch, which was lined with old-fashioned rocking chairs for everyone to enjoy. It had been such a long time since I'd enjoyed this porch.

"So, Val, even though we couldn't be more excited to have you home, what made you come back from your mission?" Nan asked. My family did not sneak around the truth. There was no point in small talk anyway.

"Well, honestly, I was having a fun time, but I struggled with the Church's history and my testimony. They tell you to think of the bigger picture, the fact that it is the one true church, and the testimony you have of Joseph Smith being a prophet. After my belief in all of that started failing, after I started questioning my testimony in my heart, I decided to leave," I responded.

"Wait, so are you not a member of the Church anymore?" Gramps quickly asked.

"I'm technically still a member in the Church, but I have decided not to practice, and I don't believe anymore."

Gramps had grown up in California before moving to West Virginia, and he knew a lot of Latter-day Saints growing up. He could not believe one was leaving, especially me, after my determined move to Arizona. I could tell Nan was a bit shocked as well. They continued to ask questions, but they knew I did not have many answers yet. We moved on to updates in Mia's life and then to talking about Mom and Paul. I sat and listened. It felt good to be quiet. I had missed so much being gone, and I just soaked everything in now that I had been welcomed back.

The late-spring breeze swept the porch of any pollen. I zoned out of the conversation and remembered all the wonderful times I'd had here, whether or not I'd realized at that time how special of a place it was.

Chapter Twelve

BECAUSE I KNEW YOU,
I HAVE BEEN CHANGED FOR GOOD

"Your vision will become clear only when you look into your heart.
Who looks outside, dreams. Who looks within, awakens."
Carl Jung

SPRING

ON MY FLIGHT TO ARIZONA that Monday morning, I decided to start a new online journal to keep a record for myself, not the missionaries.

June 5

This time two years ago, I was writing because the missionaries told me it was a promising idea. I was getting ready to leave my family and my home—for good reasons, I thought. Right now, I'm headed to Arizona again. This time it will be temporary. I'm leaving the Church, and I need to say goodbye, report my mission to the Arizona ward, and gather my things. I'm sad about all these things;

I feel as I'll be leaving a piece of my heart in Arizona. The journey helped me to figure out what really makes me happy and who I am in this big world.

I hope the Parker family isn't too hurt. I wonder what they think of me now. They seemed sad on the phone, of course, but I hope they understand. I'm a bit nervous to report my mission to my Arizona ward. They know me better; they've been there with me through this entire journey, and now I'm changing my mind. I'm nervous to confront that. I'm not ready to tell those people I don't believe in the Church anymore, but I'm doing it, and it is going to be fine.

I'm going to close out of this document now and sleep the rest of the way. It will be a long week, and I look forward to its blessings and complications. I feel more ready than ever to be who I am, and I hope that others will love me anyway. I may be nervous, but I feel confident in my decision. I'm hoping this goes well, but I also know that everything happens for a reason. It is well with my soul.

Western bound again,

Val

I was not nervous to see the Parker family. Things came naturally with Gram, Amelia, and their families. I was grateful for that. What I felt would be the most challenging was talking with my stake president and bishop. They had invested in my mission with the help of the ward members, who were touched with my conversion testimony of the gospel.

I felt like I owed them to stay a part of the Church. That was obviously not true, but I struggled with my feelings anyway. My mission while in Texas was to strengthen the members there and baptize and teach new members. I had done nine out of eighteen months of that. These people had taught me a new dedication to life and happiness. After learning what they all believed, and after believing it myself, I gained greater knowledge. I learned on my mission that true happiness lay in creating memories, moments, friendships, strong family ties; I learned to appreciate the sunsets and my front porch a bit more, to not starve myself, to be happy where I was, and to love myself and to create a life that I loved.

I was grateful to have learned these things through moving to Arizona and being baptized into the Church. But I had also learned that all those things could still happen even though I didn't believe that Joseph Smith was the prophet of the restoration of the gospel, which meant that I didn't believe the Church was true. I knew in my heart that not believing was okay.

Still, these were people with whom I had created friendships and spent the last two years of my life. These were the people I had left my family for, and I was heartbroken to disappoint them. Some of them understood and treated me kindly, and other said things such as "We know you will return to the fold" or "You are making a mistake, but we know the Lord will guide you back to the truthfulness of this gospel." I took their comments lightly. Even though I felt broken inside with the loss of so many friendships and such a strong community, I also felt relieved.

I still had the companionship of the Parker family and my own family in West Virginia. I needed nothing else. Honestly, despite what the Church officials said, I even felt the companionship of the Holy Ghost. I felt content amid the chaos. I had a lot to figure out, but I was calm for the first time in months—and I was not lying to myself in a virtual journal.

After my missionary release, the disappointments and hopes that I would return to the Church later in life faded away. I went to my favorite soda shop and taco shop with the entire Parker family. I got to laugh and sing in the car with them. I got to see another Arizona sunset. I got to drive by and see the next football team and pom squad practicing early in the summer for the fall season.

Some things you just do not have words for—you have to experience it.

The next few days flew by with packing, collecting things, taking pictures, and getting ready to go home. As much as I loved being in Arizona, I was meant to be home right now. I knew it in my heart.

Renee got off her flight, rented a truck, and pulled into the driveway of what had been my home for the year before I served my mission. She was driving a U-Haul, and we would be leaving on a cross-county trip within a few hours. The Parker family and Renee helped me load my things. Everyone was civil now, and that was a blessing, too. Before Renee and I left, we had a meal with the Parker family.

Gram prepared shredded chicken tacos with fresh grown cilantro, cucumbers, and homemade ranch dressing. I had helped her make everything that morning. I made sure she knew that she had given me a love for cooking and healthy living. She knew what I had struggled with in the past, and she truly helped me become grateful for my own body, and for the benefit of what a healthy lifestyle could do for the mind, body, and spirit.

I might not have believed the doctrine of the Church of Jesus Christ of Latter-day Saints in the end, even after genuinely believing in the beginning; but I did believe in joy, family, relationships, creation, and myself. Those beliefs were ones I would have never known, or would have realized late, without the Parker family.

I left that Wednesday morning with a heavy heart. I was leaving something wonderful. I was also headed to something mended and just as beautiful; I simply had a lot of growing to do now on the East Coast. I cried because this journey had helped me understand that every family was imperfect and that mine was just as wonderful. The Parker family had changed my life for the better.

At the time, I was rereading *Anne of Green Gables* by Lucy Maud Montgomery. I loved the character of Anne and how she lived her life with pure appreciations for education, family, and the beauty of the world around her. The book read, "Kindred spirits are not so scarce as I used to think. It's splendid to find out there are so many of them in the world." For the first time, I related to what Anne said about kindred spirits. I felt grateful to realize now that I had so many.

Our route took us through Albuquerque, New Mexico. We passed Route 66 tourism signs, charming hole-in-the-wall diners, and beautiful rocks that I could have stared at for hours (and did stare at for hours), no matter how alike they looked. We eventually reached our final stretch in the eastern panhandle of West Virginia.

Renee and I had many deep conversations while driving and a lot of laughs. We had never been close before, but she apologized for our past, and we only grew in closeness from then on. She would never be my mom, but she was a blessing in my life, and I wanted her to know that she meant a lot to me.

We pulled into the driveway at Mom's house around dinnertime and started unloading all my things. Mom lived with Paul, so I would have my own room downstairs until I figured out what my life would look like.

After unpacking everything into the house, Renee hugged me and told me that she was glad I was home for good, and that she enjoyed our trip. I agreed, and I thanked her for taking the time to get me and all my things back to West Virginia. We took a selfie together to remember the end of a wonderful cross-country trip.

"You know, Val, I wanted to hate the Parker family. Your dad and I felt as if they stole you. We all did. But after meeting them, it is like all the walls I had just broke down. They are some of the best people I have ever met. I can tell that they helped you to grow into an amazing young woman. I want to thank them one day, for everything. They've been nothing but good to you for these last couple of years, and I'm grateful you found them," Renee told me softly.

"Thank you for saying that. I am feeling very blessed. Thanks for everything, Renee. I had a wonderful time with you," I told her.

We hugged again and I told her that I would see her soon. I figured I would stay with Mom and see Dad and Renee when Mia had weekends with them.

I was exhausted, but I had not seen any of my things in so long, and Mom was eager to help. Paul was working the night shift, so Mom and I ordered from the pizza joint around the corner and began unpacking my life from the last two years.

Mom and I were generally and obsessively talented at organizing. I didn't know if it was a family trait, but when things were organized, we felt as if we had a bit of control over our worlds. Mere hours later, we had mostly finished. The last bag included all my temple garments, temple clothes, and scriptures.

"Mom, I don't know what to do with all of these," I told her.

I was conflicted. Heavenly Father might be sorely disappointed in me if I threw any of the temple garments, clothing, and scriptures away. My mom looked at what I was referencing. We were not supposed to show people the garments or temple clothes; they were sacred—although, if Heavenly Father was going to be disappointed, I figured He already was at this point.

Mom looked at me and smiled. "That's up to you, Val. I suppose you must make sure your decision to leave is permanent and go from there."

"I have decided, Mom. It's just not for me."

"Then throw them away, know you are loved anyway, and move on." She always got straight to the point, not wasting precious time. As someone who tended to overthink things, I was grateful for her candor.

We went through the sacred items that no longer meant as much to me and put them in a bag for Mom to get rid of tomorrow. Even though I did not see them as sacred anymore, I still had a connection with the stories behind them; I couldn't bear to be the one to throw them away.

The rest of the week slipped by as I visited people and hiked as much as I could in the mountains that once felt like a barrier for me. I had finally conquered them, and now anything was possible.

I decided to hike alone to one of my favorite spots in Berkeley Springs. The small town was over the mountain and in the valleys further into West Virginia. My great-grandmother Irma—or Meemaw, as I always called her—lived there. I wanted to surprise her that day. She was in her early nineties now, so I made sure I called her first to let her know I was at least home from Texas. I knocked on her door about an hour later with flowers.

She opened the door and gave me the sweetest and most gentle hug. She cried tears of joy as she told me she loved me many times before welcoming me inside.

Our visit went like those in the past. We sat facing each other across the couch as she turned her television program off. She took off her reading glasses and wrapped herself in her sweater. She was always cold. Even in June she wore her oversized, fuzzy cardigan. She was healthy for her age, and I was grateful for that. She asked me what I thought about the world, asked how I was doing, and what my plans were.

"Meemaw, I'm good. Better than I have been in a while. I have gone through a lot of changes recently, but they've all been good. How are you holding up?"

"Oh, girl, I'm fine and dandy. I'm wanting to know about you! I haven't seen you for over a year. Tell me everything."

I told her *almost* everything. There were some things about the Church and about my experience that I still had a challenging time putting into words, so I saved both of us the confusion.

She was pleased to know that I was home with my family. She never had much of an opinion of the Church until now, but she did know it took me away from my family in the grand scheme of things. She did not like that. I did not like it either after I realized that I missed them and wanted them in my life. I was glad they welcomed me back.

"So, that is it. I'm home for good now, and I'm not sure what my plans are. It is stressful, but I have a few options, and I know it will all work out"

"You are right. It will. What are your options?"

"Well, I can go to school at the local university. I don't know what I would study, though. I could get a full-time job, but I don't know where I would want to work."

"It seems like you've got a lot to figure out."

"I sure do," I said as we both giggled.

We had a wonderful visit. I had missed her old soul and beautiful, solitary way of life. She was content. She was my most kindred spirit, and I wanted to be as satisfied as she was. We hugged goodbye and I left the flowers at her table in a vase with fresh water. We hugged again, because there was no such thing as too much hugging in my family, especially after I had not seen them in so long. After telling Meemaw that I loved her, and after she told me that she was glad I was home, I went on my hike.

I drove to the hiking trail at Cacapon State Park with a heart full of joy and nostalgia. I regretted what I had missed while I was gone but was full of gratitude for what I had experienced in Arizona and Texas. My journey was necessary for growth. I sat at the mountaintop with tired legs, bright eyes, and tears flowing. I was alone and I was happy. I was genuinely happy. I had been through so much and still had so many people who loved me. I had a lot of important decisions ahead, and I needed the courage to make the right ones. I felt invincible, but I also needed guidance.

"Dear Heavenly Father, I'm coming to you in prayer, asking for your guidance. Where should I go from here? The last few years have been a roller coaster, but I know that no matter what faith I affiliate with, you are there and you love me. I'm so blessed to have that knowledge. Please bless my family and the Parker family. They deserve all the goodness in this world. I pray to be led in the way that will be best for my life. I pray that I'll learn, grow, and accept an old way of life with new eyes. Thank you for all the challenges, trials, and blessings in my life. Amen," I prayed.

I hiked down from the beautiful outlook, from which I could see Maryland, Pennsylvania, Virginia, and West Virginia. It was breathtaking, every single time. Even though there was no distinct difference between mountaintops that belonged to different state boundaries, it was thrilling to think about the history of the people, the stories, and the hikers who had seen this and felt connected to the world yet small at the same time.

I got into the car that Dad had given me upon my return. He had gotten a new one from the dealership and gladly passed along his older car. I was so grateful, and I drove with windows down and the music surrounding me as the sun glistened against the windshield, the wind blowing my hair.

Chapter Thirteen

ROOTS BEFORE BRANCHES

*"Once you replace negative thoughts with positive ones,
you'll start seeing positive results."*
Willie Nelson

SUMMER

CAMP FLEW BY, AS USUAL. A week in the mountain without cell service was always a beautiful and positive experience, and it always went by too quickly. On the last day, we woke up, did our daily activities, and met for lunch. I had a conversation with a friend of mine, Elizabeth, who I had grown up with in 4-H and who was going to the local college, Shepherd University—the same college I'd learned Jayce was attending. It was a small liberal arts institution by the river with a unique community. She was studying nursing, which was nothing I was interested in, but I asked her a lot of questions about the school.

"What made you want to go there?" I asked her over garlic bread and spaghetti.

"Well, a lot of their programs are small, which makes it easier to have experiences with professors and other students in your field. If you go somewhere like WVU, it's fun and exciting, and it is good school, but you lose that connection. Just my opinion, though. I think you'd really like Shepherd," Elizabeth answered.

"That sounds great. I've been considering it for sure. Do they have a teaching program?" I asked. I didn't know where that had come from, but I went with it. I had always liked school, and I liked writing, and teaching seemed like a good start.

"They do! I have a few friends in it. Some people here are enrolled there, too. I've heard it's a good program. You would be a great teacher, Val," Elizabeth said.

"Well, thank you! I don't know for sure if that's what I want to do, but it may be a good place to start. I thought about working full time, but I just don't know if I'm ready to commit to a company. I would much rather find a career that suits me."

"I think you're on the right track," she said as we dumped our plates and ran to the freezer in the kitchen for a popsicle. It was nearing ninety-five degrees outside, and we laughed as we cut the tops of the plastic off. Popsicles might be childish, but they were necessary on a day like this.

Elizabeth and I were not in the same 4-H camp tribe. I went to mine and she went to hers after lunch. Our tribes prepared funny skits and silly songs for the last council circle of the night. As evening settled, my tribe met on the front porch of the dining hall, then ventured onward to our nightly ceremonies as an entire camp. We hiked down to the outlook, the perfect area to see the sunset each night. The trumpet player played taps, and we all sang,

"Day is done, gone the sun,
From the lake, from the hills, from the sky.
All is well, safely rest, God is nigh."

After reflecting on the day as we watched the sun go down, we silently made our way to the council circle, where together we had a memorable and fun evening around the campfire. Each tribe showed their spirit and creativity through songs, dances, and rhymes made up throughout the day. It was an exciting and bonded atmosphere that everyone loved. At the end of the night, we sang more songs, including one of my favorites that I had forgotten from years past.

As the fire faded and the night ended, the entire camp sang the low and sentimental lyrics to end the night. The mountains themselves seemed to sing to me,

"I'm waiting for you here in West Virginia,
counting every day 'till you arrive.
There's so much in my heart I want to give you,
and there's so many mountains we can climb.
It is more than plain to see,
that you are the one for me,
so walk back through my door,
we're no secret anymore.
So, come home to West Virginia—
come hear the mountain song,
you have been away too long.
So, come to West Virginia."

"West Virginia is the place where you belong," the campers finished singing. I could not sing that night because the song brought me to tears, as it did with many other campers. I was glad I wasn't the only one feeling such overwhelming joy and purpose where I was. I believed I was really in the right place at the right time.

We ended the campfire circle, my tribe won the spirit stick for the week of activities, and the next day we all went home with hearts full of spirit and joy for the lives we were living.

Days later, I got my first tattoo. Well, I got my first three tattoos at once. Mom was excited and thought it was hilarious that I was so gung-ho to get three tattoos in one appointment. She went with me, of course. She had truly become my best friend. Mia was also there; we had gotten quite close since I came home.

I created the designs with the tattoo artist. My first tattoo went on my collarbone, reading, in cursive, "It is well with my soul." I had always loved the idea of tattoos, but the Mormons believed it was a disgrace to defile your body after you knew the truth of the Church. I disagreed. I thought they were beautiful and shared stories.

The next tattoo was a small, spunky, green four-leaf clover on my right arm, which represented my love for 4-H. I had decided it would be the only one on that arm. The final one was a twelve-inch piece running horizontal to the ulna bone in my left arm. It went from my wrist to my elbow, and it said, "Come hear the mountain song," with *mountain* replaced with a tattoo of mountains. That one made my heart smile, remembering coming home and remembering singing about it at 4-H camp.

After my long tattoo appointment, the three of us went back to Mom and Paul's house for dinner and to settle in for the rest of the weekend. Mia and I watched television and talked while we ate our dinner in my room. Mom and Paul decided to go on a motorcycle ride. It was beautiful outside.

"Want to go on a beach trip?" Mia asked out of nowhere.

I grinned. "Of course I do! But when and how?"

"Well, I figured since you'll be getting into work or college shortly, we could go maybe in a couple of days. If you have some money saved up, I'll contribute also. We can stay in a cheap hotel, and we can even go grocery shopping to save on dinner bills. We have to budget for at least one night of crabs, though."

We giggled. She was right, though; crabs were a necessary meal at the beach no matter what. We discussed our plans until Mom and Paul returned from their summer ride down the windy West Virginia roads. Mom came in and sat on my bed. "What are you girls up to?"

"Nothing much, just planning the best summer beach trip ever before everything changes again. But this time it's to celebrate Val being home," Mia said. Her comment made my heart swell. She was truly glad I was home. I was too.

Mom laughed. It was not a rude "never going to happen" laugh but rather an encouraging one. I could tell she was simply happy we were all together and planning exciting things.

"Only if I can go with you," Mom said.

"Of course you can!" Mia and I said in unison.

"I'm only kidding—I do have to work—but you two have a blast and call if you come into any trouble or questions."

Mia and I attacked her with hugs, thrilled that we could continue planning our trip.

Mom commented before she left the room, "We've all learned we have to make the most of the time we have together. Life throws so much at you, some terrible things, and a lot of good things, but the secret is to focus on the good and try to make more of it."

A week later, Mia and I loaded chairs, towels, and bags into the car for our quick last-minute beach trip. I had my morning cup of coffee and put on my sundress that exposed my shoulders and my new tattoo on my collarbone. I felt fantastic and free. It truly was well with my soul. I smiled at Mia, who had become one of my closest friends.

We waved at Mom as we rolled down the windows to welcome the eighty-degree morning, pulled out of the driveway, and I felt full of hope and peace as we drove, talked, and listened to music.

We sat silently with music playing in the background for quite a while as we continued down the coastline. I thought of throwing my garments and temple clothing away. I thought about leaving home years ago. I thought about how I had to recreate what I had ruined, but I also had hope—hope that this all happened for a reason, and that things were already falling into place.

Hours later, we crossed the Chesapeake Bay Bridge and miles

after that pulled into the hotel. We stepped out of the car and inhaled the strong, salty, wonderful air.

Something about the water made me feel so small yet so free and connected. It allowed me to realize that in the grand scheme of things, I was minuscule, and so were any problems I had. Knowing that my problems were no bigger than a few grains of sand made me feel light and connected.

The mountains had started to feel that way to me, too. I was grateful for this transformation in my thinking. It just took time and experience to realize.

We checked into our hotel for the next two nights, threw down our things, and ran to the beach, our swimsuits already on under our clothes. We sat and enjoyed the entire day, until the sun began to set.

"So, what do you think you're going to end up doing, Val?"

"What do you mean? Like, in life?"

"Yeah. I mean, sort of."

"I don't have a complete plan, but I have decided I should get a part-time job and then start school in the fall. I'll be a bit late to the college scene, but I need to go. I've been considering education."

"That would be really cool. I think you'd be a great teacher."

"Thanks, Mia. I appreciate you. I'm a bit nervous, but I sent my forms and everything a few nights ago, after I got back from 4-H camp. I just needed a bit more time to think."

"You made the right decision. I have no clue what I'm doing with my life."

I reassured her that she would do great at whatever she chose after she finished high school.

"Either way, I really am glad to have you back. I would much rather you go to college right down the road than in Arizona, anyway. And I would much rather you not be Mormon. Nothing against the Parkers. I actually think they're cooler than our family sometimes, and I love them to death, but seriously, that is all a bit crazy—the Mormon thing."

We laughed at that. I did not say much besides the fact that I agreed with her.

Mia and I had a peaceful, fun, and sunny trip at the beach. The sun shined on our faces as we talked, bonded, and made up for so much lost time.

Days later, I pulled the car into the driveway, precisely as it was when we pulled out of the driveway, with a few hundred miles tacked on.

Mia went back to Dad's house, and I stayed with Mom and Paul.

"Hey, y'all, how are you? Mia and I had an amazing time!"

"We're good. We're so glad you had a wonderful time at the beach," Paul responded.

"What did you girls get into?" Mom asked.

"Well, we mainly relaxed. Ate crabs one night, got plenty of sun, and just enjoyed being in the sand, surrounded by the salty water," I said. Mom and Paul smiled. "But I also thought quite a bit about my plans."

I told them I was going to start school at Shepherd University in the fall. Paul and Mom offered to let me continue staying with them while I studied. They were excited that I was going to school, and they called Nan and Gramps on speaker to share the news.

"That is such exciting new, Val! This is great!" Nan exclaimed.

"I agree wholeheartedly. This is good news, sweetheart. I hope you know that your nan and I will always be there for you, despite what you may think and despite the past," Gramps reassured me.

I appreciated his assurances. Gramps meant it from the heart, and we had all grown so much since my move to Arizona years ago.

"Where will you be living while you go to school?" Nan asked.

"Well, living on campus is out of the budget, unfortunately, and as much as I love it here at Mom and Paul's home, it would be about a forty-five-minute drive each day to classes. I'm just trying to scope out the options and decide which of the two are best, especially because I would not be there for the traditional college experience."

I would be older than most of the first-year students there, so I did not care much about the social aspect. I just wanted to get my degree and choose a career.

"Well, honey, just know we love and support you. We're sorry for how we behaved when you were figuring yourself out, and we hope you know how proud we are of how far you've come," Nan said.

"I'm sorry, too. And thank you for saying that; it means a lot. I love you both so much," I told them.

"We're only fifteen minutes from the school, Val. You are welcome to move into the guest room. You did grow up here, for goodness sakes. It's basically your room anyway," Gramps stated. "We would love that, Val. We've missed you."

"That means a lot, Gramps. I have missed everyone so much. I'm going to get ready for bed and begin unpacking from the beach, but I'm sure I'll be over soon to discuss this stuff and catch up," I said to them.

"That sounds good. We'll talk with you soon, dear. Have a great night with your mom and Paul. We love you guys!" Nan said to everyone.

"We love you too," we chorused in response.

Weeks later, I moved back into Nan and Gramps' home on Myers Ridge Road, where I had spent so many of my previous years. The house was filled with memories of happiness, tears, and overall goodness. I finished organizing my bed, desk, and dresser. I sat on the edge of the bed, looked around, laid back, and smiled as the fan above me blew the cool air around the room. It was about 95 percent humidity outside, so the air-conditioning felt glorious after moving everything in.

I felt like I was home in all the ways. School would begin in four weeks, and I would start my part-time job at the coffee shop downtown in two. I would only work on the weekends, and I was thrilled to make coffee and get to know people in the community.

During those two remaining weeks of freedom, I planned to go on a lot of hikes, plenty of single coffee dates, and read in my hammock any chance I got.

I did just that. I hiked many mountains alone, with only my thoughts and the sounds of nature around me. I would hike, and I would find a coffee shop and indulge with an espresso drink, then head home and read for the rest of the day in my hammock.

"Dinner is ready, Val!" Nan announced the night before I reported to my job for the first time at the coffee house. Nan and Gramps believed in eating dinner together. My whole family did, as did the Parkers. It was such a simple and beautiful thing.

"This looks delicious, Nan. Thank you so much. I call making dessert!" I told them.

"I can be alright with that," Gramps said.

We loved enjoying a cup of coffee and fresh dessert together. Nan had made fried chicken with potatoes and greens. She made a fantastic batch of fried chicken. I made a quick batch of cookies from the homemade dough I had stored in the freezer a couple of days before. I knew I would have use for it. We brewed a fresh pot of coffee and enjoyed the two together on the porch before it was time to call it a night. Gramps went in after giving me a forehead kiss and tapping our mugs together in celebration.

It was these moments—dinner and memories with my family, trips with my sister, catching up with my siblings, coffee dates by myself, truly talking with my parents, appreciating the immaculate mountains and rivers that West Virginia offered, and spending valuable time with everyone—that I did not appreciate before my journey.

I was grateful for it every day. But I also missed the Parker family every day. I did not miss the Church, but I did miss them.

I sent a quick group text to Gram and Amelia.

Hey, you two, I just wanted to let you know I've been thinking about you, and I love you. I miss your family, and I hope you know how much y'all mean to me. I took a selfie of myself with the West Virginia sunset in the background. It was almost 7:30 p.m., but the sun was just now going to sleep in my town. *Not as great as an AZ sunset, but I thought I would share it with you.*

They both texted back quickly.

Come visit soon! You always have a place to stay, Gram said.

So true! You are welcome anytime, sweet friend of mine, Amelia told me.

You two are such a blessing in my world. I don't know if I would be where I am without y'all. Thank you, I said.

I meant that.

I had heard rumors that people from high school said that my moving to Arizona, being baptized into the Mormon church, and then deciding after all that time that I wanted to come home was a waste of time. I sat on the porch of my home on Myers Ridge Road, sipped my coffee, rocked back and forth in the rocking chair, and thought about how much of a blessing the entire journey had been. I chuckled at the idea that it was a waste of time.

Thinking about it more, I cried tears of recognition for what had taken me so long to realize and understand. I was grateful beyond words for this journey. This was life, not a waste of time. I softly chuckled for a moment as I wiped my tears and sipped my coffee before heading inside to sleep.

I thought that I should write about this.

August 2

Around this time two years ago, I was about to be a baptized member of the Church of Jesus Christ of Latter-day Saints. I was thrilled because I felt as if the doctrine was an answer to my prayers, and Arizona and living with the Parker family would give me the freedom, positivity, and family I needed. I did truly need those things, but if I have learned a few things in the last two years, it is that no church is going to make you happy all the time; churches are imperfect.

God is felt in nature, in your heart if you welcome Him, and He is in the simple and beautiful things if you choose to see Him there. I have learned that you must love yourself before you can love anyone else. The Parker family showed me how to love the crazy, sometimes confusing mess that life can be. They are beautiful and wonderful. They taught me that life is what we make it, that compassion, forgiveness, and love triumph overall. I learned that I'm beautiful, fun, and full of life. I'm not the girl I used to be, who didn't feed herself, didn't love herself, and never imagined that she would be good enough.

How full of joy I am, to sit on the porch tonight where I spent so many years—at peace, finally. I never thought I would come back here and be happy about it. I never thought the mountains would feel freeing. I never thought my family would become some of my best friends. I sit here tonight, full of love and excitement for the future.

Tomorrow, I start my job at the coffee shop right outside of the university I'll be attending in two weeks. I look forward to meeting new people and starting yet another journey.

Signing off for now, until the smell of fresh coffee beans in the morning,

Val

Chapter Fourteen

WHERE YOU BELONG

"I'm not a bit changed—not really. I'm only just pruned down and branched out. The real ME—back here—is just the same."
Lucy Maud Montgomery

END OF SUMMER

MY SHIFT AT THE COFFEE SHOP was magical in its own respect. Every weekend, I walked into the stone corner store that sold fresh bakery items, fresh-brewed local coffee, espresso drinks, also lunch specials. It was a lovely, quaint establishment where free newspapers were available, local businesses posted their cards on the bulletin board, and children living nearby would buy gumballs out of the machine and pay for a bottled soda. I enjoyed learning the ropes. I especially loved smelling fresh coffee beans all day.

I worked with Kindra, a red-headed beauty who had a good head on her shoulders. She was a year younger than me, but she was also starting at Shepherd University as a first-year student in a couple of weeks. You could tell just by talking to her that she knew what she wanted out of life. I liked her. We became friends on my first day. Every shift those next two weeks at the coffee shop consisted of Kindra and I selling a lot of pastries and coffee and finding the friend in each other that both of us wanted. We were both very independent, but we liked each other's company and laughs. We went on many lunch outings, a few late-night donut runs to the small Dutch donut shop about twenty minutes away from home, and we knew everything about the other. I stayed connected with some of my friends from high school, specifically Erin and Amber, but Kindra was a newfound friend in a new stage of new life, and I was grateful for her friendship.

Our first week on campus, we learned that we had a couple of classes together. Our outings got cluttered with due dates, schoolwork, and meetings. Autumn began and we saw each other less, but I was grateful for our shifts together at the coffee shop. Coffee brought people together. I was grateful I could drink it. I drank too much, but there was no need to worry about that anymore.

I enjoyed the courses I was taking and the path I was on. I loved home with Nan and Gramps. I got to escape at the end of the long days of classes and do homework on the porch as the autumn breeze grew cooler with each day. I had a cozy setup in my room as well: pumpkin-scented candles burning, calming lighting, and all my books were back on their shelf.

Before I knew it, it was November, and my classes were finishing their hefty assignments and final exams. I drove to school on a brisk Friday morning, the last day before Thanksgiving break began. I had a couple of classes, so I parked in the lot far away and took the long way to class. I enjoyed these chilly mornings, all wrapped up with my rain boots crunching the leaves. I had decided to stop by our coffee shop and say hi to Kindra. She was working this morning and had her classes later in the afternoon.

I opened the door, and the brass bell rang as Kindra waved to me from behind the counter. We gave each other a hug, and she gave me a cup to go for my drip coffee.

"Want to come over later to bake cookies? We deserve that after this semester so far," I told her.

"I so agree. I'll be there after my classes," she responded.

"Great! I'll have fresh apple cider from the market, and a card game dealt for us to play while they bake," I said. "Have a great shift!" We tapped coffee cups.

I headed out, turned the corner to campus, and my stomach did a complete upside-down flip.

Jayce Adams was walking right toward me. *Oh Lord, help me.*

I felt helplessly discomfited. *Goodness, we haven't talked in so long, and last time I saw him, his family was at graduation for another girl. He is clearly on a different page.*

Awkwardly, he said, "Hey, Val" with a head nod toward me. I nodded back and waved helplessly, not having a clue what to say as we passed one another.

My poor stomach would not stop turning. I hated butterflies, especially when they weren't mutual. *How dare I fall into his curly-blond-hair, charming-smile trap?! Val, stop. He has a girl. Forget about it. No, no, no.*

I calmed my nerves and continued to class. But my mind was filled with Jayce—our memories, losing Thomas and how he must have felt, our talks, everything.

When Kindra finally got to my house later, *boy* did I need to vent to her about what had happened. Thankfully, I'd had some time to calm down.

"Sounds like an old flame being rekindled to me," Kindra said and giggled. She knew I agreed but that I refused to say it or further consider the thought. I gave her a huffy look before succumbing to her laughter.

"No way, Kindra. Not going to happen. I'm quite sure he has

a girlfriend, or at least he did a couple of months ago," I told her. I explained the graduation scenario.

We started baking cookies as we talked, playing music in the background and mixing the ingredients. The cold sun outside brought some warmth and plenty of light reflecting off the stained glass hanging in the window. Rainbows danced along the walls, and we danced along with them as Brooks & Dunn's "Red Dirt Road" filled the air with feel-good music that told the story of simple childhood in the country, learning about accepting people, and the goodness within all of it. Someone's life can be different than yours and still be a life worth living, and I felt as if mine was one worth living and singing about. The words spoke to my soul, and even though the song was upbeat, I felt my heart swell almost to tears.

Kindra and I sang every word in what seemed like a slow-motion moment—dancing, singing the chorus, pretending to rock the guitar for an audience while we finished the cookies and placed them in the oven in the house that may have not been down a red dirt road but was my home in the middle of the West Virginia mountains, as beautiful as ever.

Nan and Gramps walked in after they got home from work. We stopped dancing for a fleeting moment, but they followed our lead, dancing through the kitchen to give us a hug and pour their nightly glass of wine.

I loved that they did this; even after a long day of work, they took a moment to slow down and joke with Kindra and I in the kitchen and spend quality time together, drinking wine on the porch while the two of us hosted our dance party for a couple more songs and then finished our baking.

We took the cookies out of the oven, played cards, and drank cider. As we sat at the counter, my phone lit up and buzzed. Kindra and I looked at the screen at the same time. She screeched when she figured out (after quickly running away with my phone) that it was Jayce Adams texting me.

Hey Val, it's Jayce. Just wanted to let ya know it was good to see you today :) Do you think you'd maybe let me take you out to dinner sometime?

"Hey, is everything okay in there?!" Nan asked through the door to the back porch.

"Everything is fine! Love y'all!" Kindra and I called as they laughed and shut the door.

"What in the world do I say to him, Kindra?" I asked.

"Well, I think it is crucial we find out if he does have a girl first, duh," Kindra told me.

"Yeah, good point," I giggled. We looked him up on social media.

"Val, I don't see anything about that girl you mentioned," Kindra told me with a grin.

"What? He posted about Jade Ripple a while back, and he was at her graduation a few months ago," I argued.

"Yeah, well, that was a few months ago, and he took all of that down, apparently."

I took my phone back with a grin of hopefulness and scrolled through for my own reassurance.

"Text him back! But act cool," Kindra warned me.

"Yeah, we will see. Let's finish cards. I may text him back later," I replied.

"Fine, I'll finish cards as long as you promise to text him back, Val. Don't even try to ignore him like you did in high school." I had already given her a very honest version of my past with Jayce.

I winked, and she rolled her eyes and laughed. We finished our game of cards, split up the cookies, and went our separate ways for Thanksgiving break.

"I expect an update tonight, and every day until we get back from break," Kindra said as she walked off into the night. She was visiting family in another state, so she would not be back until finals week began in December.

"I promise. Love you, girl. Drive safe."

"You better! Love you too, Val. Happy Thanksgiving! I'm grateful for you," Kindra yelled to me from her car.

"So grateful for you, friend!" I yelled back as she drove away.

I took my time the rest of the night. This was a newfound trait of mine—slowing down. I did a face mask, freshened up, and put on my comfiest and warmest pajamas. I made a cup of tea and settled down in my room.

I looked at the message from Jayce. It was good to see him, but I didn't know if I should respond. *You know what? Screw it.* It *was* good to see Jayce today, and I was fine with letting him know that.

I worked up the courage to text him back. So much had changed, and that meant feeling vulnerable when talking about those changes. I did not want my heart broken.

Jayce! Hey! It was good to see you, too. I think dinner would be nice. It will be good to catch up, I typed.

Kindra said be cool; that sounds decently cool. I knew saying something was "decently cool," even in my head, was in fact not cool.

I was anxious for his reply. I wondered if he was still living around the corner at his family's home while he went to school. I wondered what he was studying. I truly did want to catch up with him.

Cool, I would like that. I know it's the holiday season, but when are you free? he asked. *Well, at least he acknowledged that going out with me would be cool. Mission accomplished. I should text Kindra.* I sent her the messages, and she sent me a video of her screaming. I, in return, sent her a video of me rolling my eyes and laughing.

Jayce and I scheduled a date for a week from that day. Kindra was thrilled, and despite my eye roll, I was excited as well.

I had not been on a date in so long. It had been two years since I'd even talked to a boy I was interested in. I did not know what to think, but I did know that it was Jayce, and I was safe with Jayce. That knowledge gave me some peace.

Everything happens for a reason, I told myself again. I began to believe that in a deeper sense than I had before.

Chapter Fifteen

DAWN AT THE END OF THE NIGHT

"Ruin is a gift. Ruin is the road to transformation."
Elizabeth Gilbert

AUTUMN, WINTER

THE NIGHT BEFORE my date with Jayce, I stayed up watching the movie *Eat, Pray, Love*. I was so inspired by the film that I quickly read the book afterward. I should have waited a sleep period or two before jumping into the book, but it was Thanksgiving break, and that was the best kind of self-love. I sat on the couch alone, painted my nails, applied a face mask, and completely faded away into the life of Liz Gilbert (Julia Roberts) as she traveled to Bali, India, and Italy via film and on the pages of the novel that Nan conveniently had on her bookshelf.

In the morning I made coffee, eggs, and pancakes to share with Nan and Gramps. Mom and Paul were over at the house, and everyone had mimosas at the kitchen table. They loved having mimosas in the morning.

"Thanks for the pancakes, Val. They are delicious. Would you like me to pour you a mimosa?" Gramps asked. I giggled, thinking he was joking. I had never had alcohol before. But he was serious, and even though I was underage by a year, it was not like we were having a morning keg party.

"Sure! I'd like to try one, Gramps. Thank you."

He came back to give me my glass.

"Cheers to new seasons, family, and gathering with love in our hearts," Mom said as we clinked glasses together.

We ate our pancakes and drank our mimosas in the kitchen in the warm house, protected from the low morning temperatures of late November. These moments that seemed to slow down held the deepest emotions for me. Sitting and laughing with my family in the kitchen, the world became magical again.

I had noticed this magic in a few other occasions: I felt it when Sarah and Mia caught me up on pop culture. I felt it when Renee and I drove cross-county together. I felt it at the beach, and at the mall with Mom and Mia. I felt it on the mountain hiking, and spending time with Meemaw. I felt it on the porch at Nan and Gramps. I had felt it so often that sometimes I felt as if I were living in slow motion, recognizing all these things for the first time. And these feelings were wonderful.

I felt the same way Liz Gilbert felt when she discovered the secret to self-love: "At some point you gotta let go, and sit still, and let contentment come to you," she realizes in the text and film. I was realizing the same thing. The contentment might not last forever, but I was content now, and that was growth.

"So, how is school, Val?" Paul asked.

"It's actually great. I'm liking it. It's mainly basic courses right now. It will be a couple of semesters until I get into the bulk of what I'm studying," I replied.

"Which is teaching, correct?" Paul remembered.

"I think so, yes," I said.

"Well, we are proud of you, Val. Truly, you amaze us," Mom told me.

Everyone nodded in agreement.

Jayce texted me, and I looked down at my phone screen.

Val, I'm excited to see you tonight. Would 5 p.m. be a good time to pick you up? We could go to dinner and grab dessert afterward. Is that okay with you? he wrote.

That sounds like a fun time. I look forward to seeing you too, Jayce, I responded.

"Oh, by the way, I'm going on a dinner date with Jayce tonight. Don't freak out. It's just a date," I quickly told my family as I tried to escape inside before they could ask too many questions. They let me flee with only a few comments and grins as I went inside to read and relax before getting ready for the night.

Mom came to my door before heading home. "Val, I hope you enjoy yourself tonight. I just wanted you to know I love you and want you to be happy. You're one of my best friends," Mom told me.

"You are one of my best friends too, Mom." I crossed my room to hug her. "Thanks for all you do."

We said goodbye until pie night, in three days. It was a family holiday tradition. We always got together as a family, even Dad, Renee, Sarah, John, and Mia. There were usually twenty people in attendance, and it took place the night before Thanksgiving at Nan and Gramps' home. Everyone showed up with appetizers, wine, and the men baked pies in the kitchen to take to their own Thanksgiving celebrations the next day while the women relaxed and caught up with each other. Once the pies were in the oven, everyone played games in the living room. It was a night of laughter, fun, and the beginning of holiday spirit.

I never looked forward to pie night much when I was in high school. I did not look forward to much back then, but I looked forward to it this year.

Send a selfie once you're ready for your date tonight! You're going to look gorgeous, Val. Miss you, friend, Kindra texted me.

I totally will. I miss you too, Kindra! Enjoy your holiday with your family. I'll keep you updated, I responded.

Having finished *Eat, Pray, Love*, I started pleasure reading *The Open Door* by Helen Keller. I cuddled into my bed, turned on my bedside table light, and opened to the bookmarked page.

"Security is mostly a superstition. It doesn't exist in nature, nor do the children of men as a whole experience it. Avoiding danger is no safer in the long run than outright exposure. Life is either a daring adventure, or nothing," I read from the pages.

I did not get much further in the book. The early sunset got the best of me. My eyelids grew heavy with thought, and I dozed off on my bed, wrapped in a blanket. I needed a nap before my date anyway, after staying up so late.

I awoke from my power nap and got ready for my date with Jayce. My stomach reminded me that I was nervous. But getting ready that night, as well as the last several years of exploring what life meant, felt like a beautiful, daring adventure. I loved my life.

I finished getting ready and took a selfie to send to Kindra. She texted several colored hearts and told me to have fun.

The doorbell rang, and I ran to get there before Nan or Gramps. I beat them to it even though they were, to my surprise, sitting patiently at the table in the kitchen.

Jayce Adams—still a quiet, lovely mess of a boy. He still had the same bright eyes full of hope and adventure and blond curls I loved looking at. Jayce made me feel as though there were no limits to what we could do in life, even though our life was quite simple.

We were no longer juniors in high school, but our love for each other was still pure and reciprocal. I had finally pushed aside my stubbornness aside.

"Hi, Val," Jayce said, his face turning red. "You look really nice. It's great to see you."

I heard the Nova roaring in the driveway. My stomach was

exploding with butterflies at this point. *Goodness gracious. Why am I getting butterflies after knowing Jayce so long?*

I concluded that this time it was real, and I was allowing it to be.

I stood in the doorway. "It's nice to see you too, and you look great. Come on in for a moment."

Jayce came in, shook Gramps' hand, and gave Nan a hug. They had met Jayce in high school, but both gave me a wink of approval. Maybe he was the right person, and this was the right time.

"What will you two be getting into tonight?" Nan asked.

"I'm going to take Val to the Blue Moon in Shepherdstown, and then I think we may swing by the donut shop for dessert. Maybe sit on your porch for a while before the end of the night, as long as that's okay with you two," Jayce responded as I shyly grinned.

"That sounds like a wonderful night," Gramps said. "You have a fun time, and be safe driving. Love you, Val!"

"I love you both! I'll see you later," I responded.

Jayce opened the passenger door to the Nova for me, and we pulled out of the driveway and drove to Shepherdstown. The Blue Moon was one of the few charming and quaint spots to eat in town. They had fantastic food, and during the summer, the patio was open and greeted guests with a natural creek than ran though the outdoor dining room with several canopy trees and giant vines. The inside was just as charming. The host led us to a corner table. I was glad to have our own little spot.

Jazz filled the room, mixing perfectly with the low murmur of conversation.

"So, what made you come home? And when did you get home?"

"The day of graduation."

"You got home that day?" he asked, surprised.

"Yes, I decided to leave the mission I was serving in Texas, and I was able to make it home for Sarah's graduation. It was important to me. But I left the mission mainly because I had learned so much about Church history that I didn't agree with."

"You mean that Joseph Smith had several wives, Brigham Young only stopped polygamy because Utah was being threatened, African Americans didn't have what they call the priesthood until a certain year, and because you realized that women can never hold any power either? According to Church history, that is."

Geez, he had done his research. He was right, so I didn't argue.

"You sure know your stuff," I giggled. "But yes, that is a lot of it. And I really started to connect again with my family and realized that according to the Church, unless they got baptized, they would not be with me after this life. The plan seemed perfect, but I began to question it. What about Thomas? I felt ridiculous that I had been so foolish as to ignore that. Just a whole host of things felt wrong about it. The Parker family, though, were so real and amazing. It was hard to leave them."

I felt bad for mentioning Thomas, but he had been on my mind lately, too.

"That is crazy. I bet. You did say they were down-to-earth and honest people," Jayce added.

"They are the only thing I miss about the whole thing."

"Do they still talk to you? I heard it's quite hard to leave that church and keep relationships."

"When did you do all this research?"

"When you and I were still writing each other. I thought you might come home."

"I see. Well, yes, we still talk. It is a bit different now that I'm not associated with the Church. But they're my family, too. I'm so grateful for them. They taught me how to love life, family, and those you choose to have in your world."

"It sounds like even though it was crazy at the time, the whole thing made you stronger and happier."

"Definitely," I said as I sipped my drink. We ordered our food and talked nonstop until it arrived.

"So, what are you studying at Shepherd?" I asked him.

"Vet science," he said unenthusiastically. "I like it, but I really don't like school. Thomas and I were supposed to do all that college stuff together. What about you?"

"English education right now. I don't know if it's what I want to do, but I like it."

"Yeah, it is hard to know, but I think you'll be great at that."

"And I think you'll be great with vet science, Jayce. Or anything you're passionate about."

"Thank you," he said as the server placed our food down.

We thanked the server, ate our food, Jayce paid for dinner, and then we got back in the Nova for a donut run. The old Dutch donut shop's lights flickered as a welcoming smell greeted us. The shop reminded me of a candy store; you could not stay too long without your teeth hurting.

We chatted, laughed, ate our donuts, and began our drive home to Myers Ridge Road. After pulling into the driveway, we migrated to the front porch. I sat in the white rocking chair next to him while the chilly November breeze curved around us. This time, we were wrapped in blankets that smelled of Nan's pumpkin candles, and there were no tears.

"Last time we were on this porch, it wasn't the greatest of nights," Jayce joked, as if he could read my mind.

"Yeah, that was an interesting time. I hated it here, you know," I told him.

"Oh yes, we all hated it here. You're just the only one who left and became a Mormon while you were at it."

"Jayce!" I giggled. He really didn't take many things seriously if he didn't have to. I loved that about him. *Heck, I love everything about him.*

"I was chasing something bigger," I added. "I thought I found it, and in a way, I did—but it wasn't what I thought. So, I came home. Do I get credit for that?"

"Totally. Pretty cool you came back. It was wild to run into you at school," he said.

"It was so great to see you. Sorry I was awkward. I just thought that you and Jade were sort of a thing, so I was conflicted," I told him.

"We were, sort of, but if I'm being totally honest, as horrible as it sounds, I didn't feel much about her after seeing you at the graduation. I didn't want to lead her on. You were back, and I had a little bit of hope," he told me.

"Why didn't you reach out?" I asked without thinking. I felt rude, but I knew he wouldn't think that, so I pushed it aside. I needed to get used to feeling comfortable; Jayce was a mystery, yet comforting and nonjudgmental.

"I knew you were probably going through a lot if you were back. I figured I would give you time. If it was meant to be, it would happen. You know?"

"Totally." I grinned and wrapped my blanket a bit tighter.

"I'm glad you're home, Val."

"Me too, Jayce. Me too."

This was home, and I was grateful that I realized that now. The temperature dropped a few degrees as the night went on. Jayce and I talked for hours on the porch. Finally I told him that I had stayed up quite late last night, and that I was getting sleepy.

He stood, walked over to me, and wrapped me in his banket, holding me close.

"I had a great night, Val. Missed you, crazy girl."

"I missed you too," I said, looking up at him.

It was then that Jayce kissed me. He kissed me gently, and it assured me that this was the first of many porch talks, late-night kisses, and adventures together.

Jayce kept kissing me, and I kept kissing back. It felt good to be so close to him and to finally kiss him after all this time. I giggled and hugged him, telling him I would see him soon.

"Would you like to come to pie night on Wednesday?"

"I remember you talking about pie night occasionally in high school. Not sure really what it is, but yes, I would love to."

"Okay, great! I'll see you then. Don't worry. I'll give you all the details. Let me know when you're safely home."

Jayce kissed me one more time and started up the Nova for the journey around the corner. I waved as he drove away into the dark night.

Alone in my room after Jayce left, this time I was content and full of joy. We would never have any idea what the future held, but we did know that we had chosen each other, and our hearts were full of simple love, imprinted with smiles.

I got home safe, Jayce texted five minutes later.

I'm glad. I had an exciting time. Thank you for everything. See you soon! I responded.

So, pie night on Wednesday. Wear whatever makes you comfortable. I'll have all the ingredients for you to make your pie (Nan said I could help you this year since you're new to the holiday), I texted Jayce the next morning.

Sounds fun! Missing you.

I grinned and told him the same. We were finally both, at the same time, embracing each other. It was all wonderful, exciting joy and goodness.

The next two days flew by, and it was Wednesday.

"What kind of pie are we making?" Jayce asked me as he arrived.

"I figured a classic apple would be fun. You can take it back to your family for your family Thanksgiving."

Jayce hugged everyone who was there, and when Dad, Renee, John, Sarah, and Mia got there, Jayce shook Dad's hand and hugged everyone else. Jayce had mentioned that he was nervous. I told him that even though my family was unique and sometimes crazy, they were loving and always in good spirits.

Nan welcomed everyone with champagne flowing and cheers all around. Pie night had been a family tradition with Nan and Gramps since before I was born. Nan always tried to get me to bring someone to the celebration, but I had not been interested in doing so. She winked at me from across the room.

"What a great tradition. Thank you all for being here this year. May your holiday season be bright, full of love, and include plenty of tasty food. Let the pie making and celebration begin!" she toasted.

I was standing next to Dad, and I gave him a side hug. I had missed him and was glad everyone was here. Everyone raised their glasses, and then men began making their pie crusts and fillings. The kitchen quickly became warm, with feet shuffling around and flour covering every surface. I poured Jayce a glass of wine. We could have a couple of glasses tonight, according to Nan and Gramps, if Jayce stayed on the couch and did not drive home.

I began slicing, peeling, and chopping the fresh apples for our pie. I loved baking, and Nan had bent the rules to help Jayce feel comfortable for his first pie night. I was grateful she had. I made the filling; Jayce made the crust. I split off for a few moments while Jayce was in the kitchen with Dad, waiting for their pies to bake in the oven.

I sat with all the ladies in the living room until it was time to start playing a game. Jayce and I were on our third glasses of wine, and we sat close to each other on the edge of the fireplace. Gramps oversaw the game while all the pies made their way through the oven and cooling process. I zoned out during yet another slow, memory-worthy moment. I wished I could do this all the time or on demand.

"Alright, everyone, so this year we are playing the headband game, where you have to give clues to your teammates to see how many cards they can guess before the timer is off. The teams are going to be men against women. The cards sit on the band on your forehead, and whichever team gets the most points at the end for how many they guessed correctly wins," Gramps explained. "I may need another glass of wine for this one," he added with a laugh.

Everyone filled up their glasses, got plates of appetizers, and split into gendered teams according to Gramps' instructions. Jayce winked at me from across the room. Dad assured me he would help Jayce. My family often saw each other's embarrassing moments as cause for making a joke or a scene, and while it was usually humorous, I did not want it happening to Jayce.

Jayce looked at me whenever he could, and I knew that because I was doing the same. The game was fun, and the girls' team won. The men went to check on their pies, which ended up looking wonderful. Everyone had one more glass of wine, talked a bit more, and then everyone got ready to go home, taking their pies with them, per tradition.

Once the house was empty for the night, Jayce and I began to clean up for Nan and Gramps. They were pleased.

"Jayce, will you be staying on the couch tonight? I know you only live around the corner, but I would rather you stay here safely until the morning," Nan told Jayce.

"I can do that. Are you sure that's all right? It has been a great night. Thank you for welcoming me into your home," Jayce responded.

"Anytime, sweetheart. I'm glad you and Val are spending time together. We are glad she is back," Nan said.

"I completely agree," Jayce said. Nan and Gramps gave us both hugs and headed to their room. Jayce and I finished cleaning in the kitchen.

"Your pie turned out great. Thanks for coming tonight," I told Jayce.

"I think it did too! Best classic apple pie in the room. I would not have missed it. I've learned to make the most of the times we have, you know?" Jayce said.

"I agree. I'm hoping we have a lot of time together."

"I would have to agree with that," Jayce said as he made his way over to my side of the sink, grabbed my waist, and kissed my lips. I would never get tired of Jayce Adams or his kisses.

Jayce and I kept kissing all the way back to my room. We closed the door softly behind us, and the two of us lay in my bed, the closest we had ever been. Jayce held me while we slept for a couple of hours. Then I got Jayce a blanket and a pillow and settled him on the couch in the living room. I turned off all the kitchen lights, blew out all the candles, and told him I would be in my room if he needed anything. He kissed me one more time, we hugged for a moment, and I left for my room with that same feeling of butterflies, warmness, and goodness.

I woke up to the smell of coffee being made. Jayce opened my bedroom door with a cup and came to my bedside with the hallways still dark and the rest of the house asleep.

I rolled out of bed and thanked him. He asked if I wanted to sit on the porch and talk before he went home.

Autumn mornings in West Virginia were easily one of my favorite things, and I recognized that now. I did not realize that adding Jayce to the moment would make it even more wonderful. Or rather, I had known that ever since high school, but I'd fought against that knowledge. I hadn't let many people be a part of my life to this extent, and I was glad that I had pushed stubbornness aside after all this time.

School would start back up in a couple of days. The holiday and the time away from school passed quickly. It was a beautiful time of family, friendship, and food.

Chapter Sixteen

THE MAGIC OF WINTER AND WEST VIRGINIA

"Alone we can do so little; together we can do so much."
Helen Keller

WINTER

I FELT LIKE I HAD gotten a breath of fresh air when I went back to classes after Thanksgiving. It was much needed, and I felt renewed.

I had one final assignment for the last two weeks of my education class, which overall had been a beneficial introduction to the teaching field.

"Your last assignment for the semester will be a page-long essay of your personal life philosophy followed by a two-page paper discussing your personal education theory. I posted the rubric and the assignment online. Does that sound achievable?" the professor asked.

The class unanimously decided that the answer was yes, and many of us looked forward to this assignment. It was a pleasant surprise among the host of essays, finals, and projects I had to complete for other courses. We would not meet until the essay was due, but until then we had time to work on it.

I began working on the assignment at once. Otherwise, for the two weeks left of school, I spent time with my family, some time alone, and the rest of my time with Jayce. I enjoyed being with him. On the last day of classes, I put the finishing edits on my paper and turned it in. All my other projects, papers, and final exams were finished. I left the building that most of my classes were in and walked to my car in the white snow just beginning to blanket the grounds of Shepherdstown. It was a magical little scene. I took a moment to watch it, staring up at the sky like a crazy person.

I had finished my first semester at college successfully, and I felt positive about all my decisions.

I texted Jayce to ask when we could meet up and spend time together during the snowstorm rolling in. Before leaving campus to head home, I stopped by the German Street Marketplace—the most quaint, warm, and beautiful-smelling place in town. I wanted to pick up a few things before hunkering down.

The bell on the back of the door and the owner greeted me upon my entrance. The original floors from the early 1900s creaked as I made my way past the organic herbs, soaps, and candles. They had a big selection of coffee. I found the one I wanted, had it ground at the front counter, and stuck around for a few moments to soak in the smell. I was almost sad to leave this incredible place. I also purchased a pine-and-vanilla soap bar and a frosted cranberry candle. I was thrilled it was Christmas, and I wanted to treat myself for making it through this semester.

I got home and started the coffee pot with my favorite peppermint-flavored light roast as the snow continued to fall outside. Sitting at the bench near the large bay window in the front of the house, I watched the trees pile up with snow, I watched my black coffee steaming, and I watched the twinkle of the Christmas tree in the reflection. West Virginia was magical. Home was magical.

No matter how much coffee I drank, I could still fall asleep anywhere, especially in a house as cozy as Nan and Gramps'. I dozed off and was startled from my nap by Nan and Gramps coming home from work. Then Mom and Paul came over for a cocktail, knowing that it had been my last day of classes for the semester.

Jayce soon came too, with a skillet full of fresh biscuits and gravy. Gramps, a lover of the Southern goodness, gladly took it and invited Jayce inside. Nan popped it in the oven to heat up for all of us to share. Then she turned to us.

"Hey, everyone, listen up! Gramps and I have an announcement," Nan announced. "Go ahead, honey."

"Well, it's nothing too dramatic, but we do have to change our street name. Because of the house beginning construction a couple of acres down from us, we can't be a continuation of Myers Ridge Road anymore. But they are letting us choose what our road is called. Nan and I have decided to name it Vita Felice Court."

"That sounds fancy," Mom commented.

"What does Vita Felice mean, Frank?" Paul asked.

"I'm glad you asked, Paul. We picked it because it means 'happy life' in Italian. Cheers to our happy life. We want this house to always be here, as a family gathering place. It is in this that we have found our truest happy life. Let us give thanks and raise a glass to the glorious mess that life is," Gramps added, getting emotional.

My entire family grew teary eyed. I must admit, I was with them. Gramps' explanation of the new street name was perfect.

While we waited for the biscuits to bake and the gravy to heat, Mom and Paul stayed in the kitchen with Nan and Gramps, and Jayce and I went to the living room to play cards. After hours of celebrating, drinking, eating, and being together, Mom and Paul went to the garage to go home for the night. As the garage doors lifted, all the snow piled against it collapsed inside. They could barely see the tires of the truck, which was now buried. Jayce's car was also buried.

Jayce and Paul worked together to clear the driveway. I ran inside to put on my ski pants, threw on a hat that warmed my ears, and ran out to meet them. The three of us had cleared the driveway hours later and then briefly warmed up by the fire in the house. It was dark by now, and things were beginning to freeze.

Jayce texted me when he got home safely, as did Mom and Paul.

My world was simple. I was still sorting out my religious beliefs, with so many pieces of different doctrine in my mind, but I wore a smile on my heart. I was all right with not knowing. I loved my simple life. I also loved how it seemed to slow down a bit during the wintertime. Winter had a clever way of bringing our attention to our blessings and giving the gift of a new year. I had not appreciated the beauty of it before my journey.

Once the snow began to melt a couple of days later, I finished my Christmas shopping. The holiday was less than a week away. I liked to go shopping by myself. I would grab a coffee, listen to as many songs in the car on repeat as I wanted, and I could take my time finding exactly what I needed. It was a kind of therapy, especially when looking for others.

I finished later that night and went home to begin wrapping. I brought all the gifts into the house from the car and sat at my desk, surrounded by a physical mess, distracted. I smiled as I remembered what gifts resided in the bags strewn about my room.

I had never felt so much peace in such a messy situation. I had changed, and it was for the better. I, for the first time in my life, was able to smile amid the chaos. That was growth.

Then, it was Christmas Eve.

Chapter Seventeen

'TIS THE SEASON

"Christmas is tenderness for the past,
courage for the present, hope for the future."
Agnes M. Pharo

WINTER

I WOKE UP and began getting ready for Christmas Eve dinner and the annual celebration that I had missed mentally and physically the previous two years.

After showering and prepping dessert, I started wrapping gifts. My family always celebrated Christmas on the eve of the holiday. We enjoyed the nighttime, and typically, like on Thanksgiving, family members had other family to see on the day itself. Having eve celebrations in November and December added a unique aspect to the holidays. I liked how we did things immensely.

For everyone this year, I took my time creating and buying gifts that came from my heart. I had a vision for gifts that would highlight exactly what I didn't appreciate before my journey. These gifts would not only be nice materialistic things but would also stand for the things that I appreciated most about my relationship with each of my loved ones.

I wrapped them all with the same smile in my heart. Before I knew it, I was putting on a nice outfit as family began to arrive.

I snuck out to go pick up Jayce as people mingled, hugging and celebrating the giving season. I started the car and let it warm up for a moment. As I pulled out of the driveway, I turned on the Christmas radio station and drove approximately seven minutes to Jayce's house.

The house was dark, quiet, yet cozy. I reminded myself that many people went to bed at this time in preparation for Christmas morning. Jayce came out and hopped into my warm car.

"Merry Christmas Eve, darlin," Jayce said charmingly as he reached over to kiss me.

"Merry Christmas, Jayce. You look nice," I told him.

"Thank you. So do you. My family wants to know if you would like to come over for Christmas dinner tomorrow," Jayce asked. We pulled out of the driveway and headed back to Nan and Gramps' house.

"That'd be lovely. I'll be a bit nervous, but I would love that," I responded.

We had time to sing along with a Christmas song on the drive. Jayce held my leg near my knee, which made me grin. I turned the car off, and we braced for the cold, freezing temperatures for a moment before running for the front door.

We busted in on an echo of laughter, cheer, and warmth as the fireplace roared, the music played, and the drinks flowed. We took our shoes off and threw them on the doormat to dry. Jayce rubbed my arms quickly to warm me up, and I did the same thing to him as we giggled.

"Want to go say hi to everyone?" I asked.

Jayce and I went around the room to greet and hug Dad, Renee, Sarah, Mia, John, Nan, Gramps, Mom, Paul, some visiting family members, and a few of Nan and Gramps' friends who were joining in our celebration.

"All right, everyone," Nan joyfully called out to get everyone's attention. "As you know, we have a family tradition here on Christmas Eve."

Many of us snickered, knowing what she was referring to. One of our Christmas Eve traditions included assigning numbers to sing "The Twelve Days of Christmas."

"Okay, everyone gather around to begin," Nan said. "As many of you know, you sing your assigned day of Christmas just like in the song. It's like a round-robin. It's a lot of fun. Gramps will begin as the first day, and we'll go from there. Ready, go!"

Somehow, the song always sped up by the time we reached twelve and moved our way back to one for the last chorus. The breathless performance ended with clapping and cheering.

"Time for gifts and dessert! Grab what you'd like to enjoy, and everyone can find a spot in the living room again," Nan directed. I hoped that everyone would love their gifts.

Jayce loved his photo from homecoming and his new hoodie that I made sure he knew I would be borrowing.

"Thank you, Val. And here is your gift," Jayce said, handing a large bag to me.

"You didn't need to do that Jayce," I said. I started to open it with a smile.

"I wanted to, and I liked figuring out what to get you. I want you to know how much you mean to me, Val," Jayce said.

I opened the gift and saw a beautiful new handbag. Inside the bag was a shadow box of two photos of us from high school, surrounded by the phrase *Love never fails.*

I teared up and hugged Jayce, thanking him for the gorgeous and thoughtful gift.

Nan and Gramps enjoyed the books that I bought them. They had mentioned wanting them, and they had taught me how important it was to slow down and do things that mattered. Mom cried over the "Stay Wild" shirt I found for her when looking at local boutiques. I liked the shirt and the message. I knew it was the perfect gift for her. I loved her tenderness about the world and her ability to be herself.

Dad and Renee appreciated their photo of the six of us—Dad, Renee, Mia, John, Sarah, and me. Paul thanked me with a hug for the herbs, spices, and blends I had found to abet his fondness of cooking, and cooking well. Everyone in the room received a beautiful gift of some kind. Everyone knew they were loved and thought about this season. I received three new books that I wanted, comfortable pajama pants, and some wonderful candles.

While the temperatures outside plummeted and the frost gathered, we sat, talked, and drank cheerfully that Christmas Eve night—the first one I had deeply appreciated.

I gazed into the twinkling lights on the Christmas tree; they captured me. I felt gentle, and hopeful. Silent, I rested my back against the stone beside the fireplace. Jayce came over with chocolate-covered pretzels, one for him and one for me, waking me from my short daze with a gentle hand, gorgeous smile, and delicious treats. We enjoyed them by the fire together while everyone slowly gathered their coats, shoes, and gifts. They were sent off with a "be safe," "text us when you get home," and a "Merry Christmas."

Soon, everyone was on their way home. Nan, Gramps, Jayce, and I were the only ones left. Nan and Gramps told us good night and, leaving the fire for us to tend to, turned off all the lights besides the Christmas tree.

"Thank you for spending Christmas Eve with us, Jayce. And, Val, we are glad you're home tonight and always," Nan said.

"Totally agree!" Gramps yelled from their room.

"Thank you for inviting me. It was wonderful," Jayce responded.

Nan and Gramps shut their door, and I received a text from Mom saying that she and Paul had gotten home safe. I got a text from Dad shortly after. Soon everyone was snug at home. Jayce and I stayed by the fireplace and talked as the night wore on. It got quite warm, and we backed away from the fire just a bit.

"What do you think the meaning of life is?" Jayce asked.

"That is quite a random question. Tell me why you thought of that while I ponder my answer," I said.

"I don't know. Just been pretty happy lately and was wondering if that's what life's all about or whatever." He was always short on words—not because he was not intelligent but because he did not want to be vulnerable.

"Hmm. You, Jayce Adams, are a gentleman of mystery."

"I wonder about the world."

"I wonder about the world, too. I like that we can wonder together," I told him. Then I gave him my answer. "Once you find the things that make your heart smile, that is when you know you have found the right things. I think being able to recognize what those things are in your life, sticking close to them, and doing what you can to keep those things in your heart—that is when you've found the meaning of a worthwhile life."

Jayce sat for a minute before commenting. "I agree. Do you think I'm a right thing?" Jayce would never say "Do I make your heart smile," but I knew what he meant. I grinned.

"Right person, and right time."

Jayce did pop a grin at that comment. "Totally agree." The grin was enough to let me know how he felt; however, I appreciated his thoughtful comments. We both loved an enjoyable conversation. We were so different in so many ways, but we agreed on what was important. And we respected each other.

"It's coming down hard out there," Jayce said.

"I didn't even realize it was snowing! Let's go!"

"No offense, Val, you know I love a good adventure, but I'm not having a snowball fight or anything crazy right now."

"Oh, you are crazy! I was not talking about that. Let's grab blankets, sit on the porch, and watch it."

Jayce laughed. "I can do that."

We grabbed drinks, blankets, and each other's hands. Outside, the chilly air bit our skin as we bundled into the rocking chairs and scooted as close together as we could. We were completely quiet for several minutes, watching the flakes tumble.

"Remember the night you left?" Jayce asked, sipping his drink. "The night I ran over here—it reminds me of this night in a way."

"Yes, I remember it quite well. The rest of the journey seems very blurry and confusing, now that I look back on it. But there are a few defining moments, that being one of them," I added. "I sure hope you don't mean it reminds you of the confusion, tears, and sadness that accompanied that night."

"Not even close. I ran over because of the stars. They were insane. Biggest and brightest I had ever seen."

"I don't remember the stars that much . . ."

"That is a shame. They were marvelous. I wish you had noticed them and remembered them," Jayce said.

"I wish I had noticed and remembered a lot that perhaps I should have all along."

"You're the one that always tells me everything happens for a reason."

"I guess you're right about that one. Still feeling like I missed those stars."

Jayce continued, "The stars, they reminded me of that. They reminded me of the fact that everything happens for a reason when I couldn't understand you leaving, Val. There is always a way."

The stars had given Jayce hope that one day I would be the right person and it would be the right time. And the stars told us that there was a meaning to life, one bigger than we knew at the time. I did not notice the stars when I was eager to leave for the West. I was much too distracted to see the beauty glowing right in my face the entire time. I was blind to the brightness, hope, and love that existed in my world.

However, this night, on the porch with Jayce, I noticed the stars glowing on the newly named Vita Felice Court. It may have taken years to notice, but the stars were big and bright to me. They glimmered in our eyes as I took in all the wonderful feelings and hope for years to come, here with my family. I was home, I was happy, I was truly healthy, and I was head over heels in love with Jayce.

"Want to fall asleep by the fire tonight and watch a Christmas movie?" Jayce asked seriously.

"Only a corny Hallmark one, though," I said.

"Absolutely not. Classics only."

I was all right with that.

"I love you, Jayce," I said nervously. "I just want you to know that."

"Val, I have missed you more than you know. I hope you know how much of my world I felt like I was losing when you left. I love you, Val Beckley—more than anyone."

With each thing this boy said and did, I fell even deeper in love with him. I learned to love life that way, too. *Cheers to new beginnings and to what the stars taught me about my most wonderful, happy life.*

SPRING

As spring began, Jayce and I visited Berkeley Springs to kayak further into the heart of West Virginia. The rivers and valleys of the Cacapon River area were beautiful, rich in history, and appropriate for the celebration of something as wonderful as spring. As the many shades of green exploded on the trees from riverbanks to mountaintops, we drove into the small town of Great Cacapon, filled with hopes engendered by the new season.

With a population of just over 460, Great Cacapon rarely had cell phone service and hosted a couple of churches, some of the most breathtaking views, and one country store and deli. The closest grocery store was thirty minutes away. We drove through, admiring the drive, then put our kayaks in the river to begin our adventurous day on waters that could be difficult to find; they were hidden and mysterious and supplied rare clear water for enjoyment. Many rivers were now flooded with brown, green, and muddy shades—still beautiful in their own regard, but the Cacapon was special.

Jayce enjoyed the clear waters because it made fishing a bit easier and more exciting. The section we were visiting was once inhabited by several Native American tribes, including the Saponi and Delaware, the Shawnee, the Mingo, and the Cherokee. Jayce and I were the only ones on the river that day. I floated ahead on my kayak while Jayce pulled in and released several rock bass and smallmouth bass.

I was deep in thought while the river carried us closer to the end point, the sun shining on the crystal waters. *I'm so blessed.* I looked back at Jayce as I prepared to go through a white water rapid.

"I love you, Jayce!" I yelled to him as I waved and prepared my paddle. I laughed aloud as the rapids threw me through the rush, giggling with joy, hope, and pure happiness—even in the chaos. Always through the chaos.

"I love you too, Val!" Jayce returned as he waved a rock bass on his thumb and threw it back into the water with a smile.

What a beautiful and wonderful life. As I broke past the rapids, I gazed up at the tallest mountain, listening to the river rushing behind me. I could almost hear the beating drums of heritage, history, and beauty; I watched the birds and deer getting their seeds and nuts from the shorelines, and one large bald eagle swooping from the sky to catch a fish in front of me. I'm sure we were both fine with the eagle having the fish instead of Jayce.

You cannot recreate this. This is raw nature in its most glorious form. How lucky we are to be here, today, together, experiencing this. This, all the things I have experienced, this is what life is about. Through its confusion, trials, and beauty, there are unmanufactured marvels, love, and there are the stars that led me back home—home to what I once thought was a dead end but is now a hopeful and bright future, full of plentiful mountains to climb.

ACKNOWLEDGMENTS

"THANK YOU" CANNOT fully express my gratitude to those who have helped get me to the point of publication for *The Stars on Vita Felice Court*. To me, this is still surreal, but I am immensely grateful and feel so overwhelmingly blessed to have such a wonderful support system.

Most importantly, thank you to my family. I don't have the words to share my proper appreciation, but I couldn't have done this without the support of each of you who read with an open mind and helped me get to this point. Our lives together have inspired this novel, which I hope touches families all over the world. Family can be a messy thing, but I truly am blessed to have the greatest one of all. I am beyond grateful to have a family that I call my dearest friends.

To my husband, Tyler, I love you and I love our story. You are my best friend, and I am grateful for your encouragement through this process.

Thank you to Greg Fields—you believed in the novel ever since I only had one chapter written years ago.

Thank you also to the Koehler Books team that made my first publishing experience a helpful and collaborative one.

Let us be thankful for now, hopeful for the future, and loving toward the past.